I0822543

Peyote Wolf

A Fernando Lopez Santa Fe Mystery

PEYOTE WOLF

A FERNANDO LOPEZ SANTA FE MYSTERY

JAMES C. WILSON

Sunstone books may be purchased for educational, business, or sales promotional use. For information please write: Special Markets Department, Sunstone Press, P.O. Box 2321, Santa Fe, New Mexico 87504-2321.

Book and cover design › R. Ahl

ISBN 978-1-63293-423-9 (hardcover)

eBook 978-1-61139-600-3

Library of Congress Cataloging-in-Publication Data

Names: Wilson, James C., 1948- author. | Wilson, James C., 1948- Fernando Lopez Santa Fe mystery ; 1.
Title: Peyote wolf / by James C. Wilson.
Description: Santa Fe, New Mexico : Sunstone Press, [2020] | Series: A Fernando Lopez Santa Fe mystery | Summary: "When a Santa Fe gallery owner is murdered during a peyote ceremony, Detective Fernando Lopez of the Santa Fe Police Department launches an investigation that exposes the cultural and ethnic fractures in Santa Fe society and takes him into the dangerous underworld of the black market in stolen Native American artifacts"-- Provided by publisher.
Identifiers: LCCN 2020022135 | ISBN 9781632933072 (paperback) | ISBN 9781611396003 (epub) | ISBN 1632933071 (paperback)
Subjects: LCSH: Lopez, Fernando (Fictitious character) | Murder--Investigation--Fiction. | Black market--New Mexico--Santa Fe--Fiction. | LCGFT: Detective and mystery fiction.
Classification: LCC PS3623.I58485 P49 2020 | DDC 813/.6--dc23
LC record available at https://lccn.loc.gov/2020022135

WWW.SUNSTONEPRESS.COM
SUNSTONE PRESS / POST OFFICE BOX 2321 / SANTA FE, NM 87504-2321 /USA
(505) 988-4418 / FAX (505) 988-1025

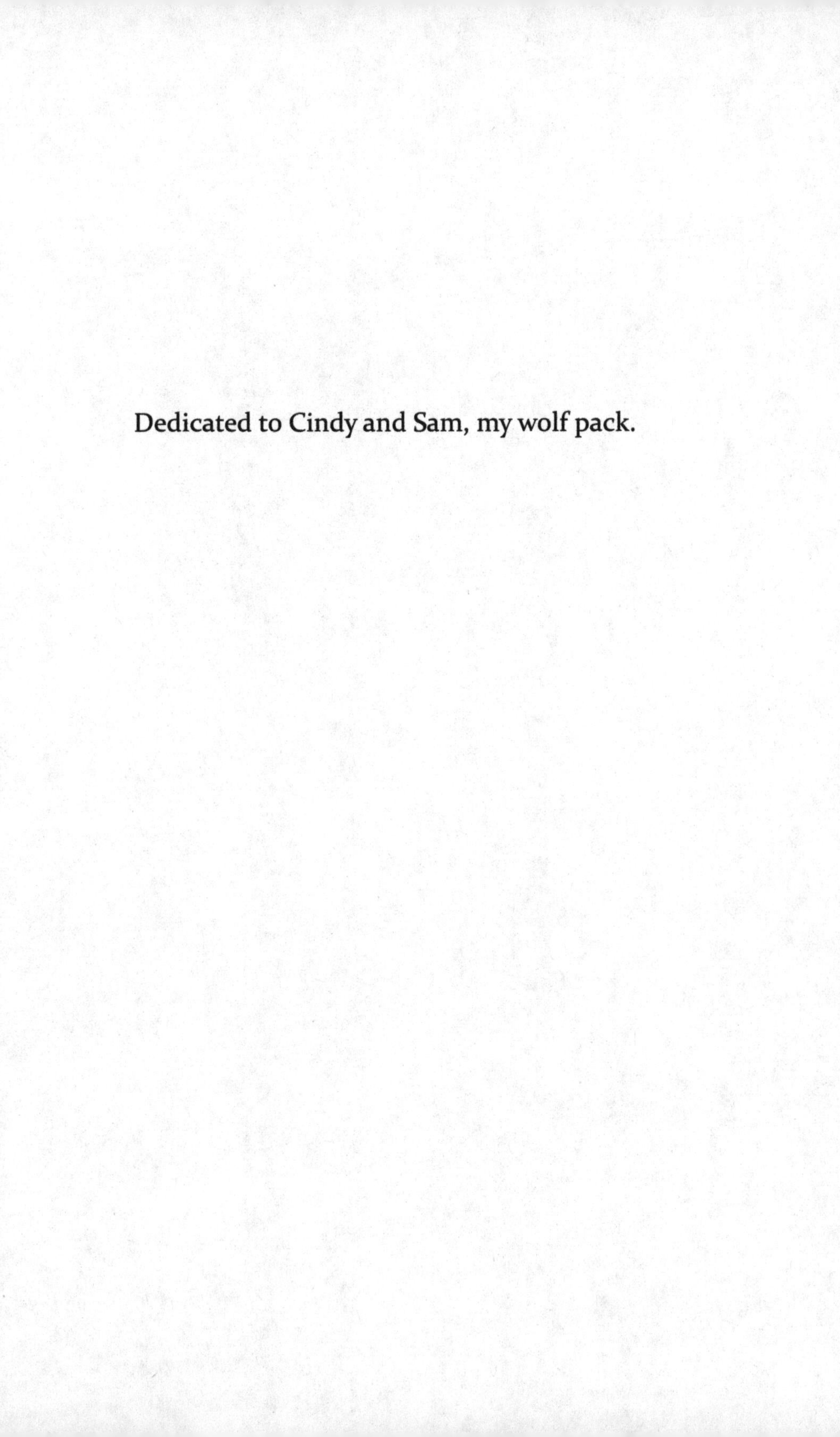

Dedicated to Cindy and Sam, my wolf pack.

Preface

I came of age reading the detective novels of Dashiell Hammett and Raymond Chandler. I loved how these stories evoked a sense of place, especially Raymond Chandler's Los Angeles. Chandler's *The Long Goodbye* is still one of my favorite novels. I also loved how these novels could reveal the fractures in the societies they represented: that is, the cultural, ethnic, and class conflicts that divided people.

Living in Santa Fe during the 1970s provided me with much the same material and inspiration. During that turbulent decade the entrenched Hispanic social and political fabric of the city came under siege by an influx of wealthy Anglos from the East and West coasts and from a wide variety of activists and revolutionaries demanding change and seeking power. Among these groups were *La Raza* and Native American activists and the counterculture movement personified by Dennis Hopper and his followers who invaded Northern New Mexico. I sometimes refer to this decade as the "fighting seventies."

Peyote Wolf, the first of my Fernando Lopez Santa Fe mysteries, attempts to expose some of the social fractures that still exist in Santa Fe while telling a whopper of a tale.

The Peyote Ceremony

Michael Soto took the bag of peyote from Cedar Chief. He chewed one brown button and passed the bag to the next person in the circle, a woman whose face was partly concealed by a red shawl. Road Chief sat in the rear of the teepee leading the ceremony with his eagle-bone whistle and bag of sage. Taking them down Peyote Road.

The fire provided the only light in the teepee. Fire Chief poked and prodded the coals, then tossed another piñon stick on the fire. He watched the smoke drift up to the open flap in the top of the teepee and dissolve into the blackness. Beyond the opening he could see a patch of night sky, the stars framed by the ends of the teepee poles. As the fire hissed and snapped, the woman beside him began to moan and rock from side to side. Diagonally across the teepee, an Indian boy sitting next to Fire Chief slumped back against the canvas with his eyes closed. The young man from San Ildefonso Pueblo might prove a useful connection in the future.

Road Chief stood, a tall ungainly man with red hair and a handlebar mustache. When Road Chief blew his whistle and began to sing, Drummer Chief joined in, shaking his rattle and beating the ceremonial drum slowly at first, then faster.

It was then he noticed that Road Chief's wife, who served as Peyote Woman, wasn't singing. Instead, she was staring directly at him. Did she know he was only pretending to sing along?

Suddenly he felt nauseous, the peyote beginning to take effect. With his eyes closed, he lost all sense of time. His mind skipped over certain moments, then stuck on others. He heard singing and drumming and talking and the constant background noise of the fire crackling and the bodies shifting on the sand.

He didn't open his eyes until he felt someone touch his left arm, an excruciating sensation. Trying to focus, he saw Cedar Chief passing a small bag of sage. He took a pinch of the dusty green leaves and rubbed it on his arms. He felt another wave of nausea swell in the pit of his stomach.

The attacks of nausea were what he hated most about the ceremonies, but somehow he always managed to suffer through them. Truth was, the peyote meetings were essential to business. Many of the tribal objects he sold in his Santa Fe gallery came from the locals he met at the meetings. So he doubled over and waited for the feeling to pass.

Gradually his perception shifted. He sensed movement around him, gradually becoming aware of the silence in the teepee. How long since the singing had stopped? He decided it must be midnight, time for the ceremony known as the Midnight Water Call.

Confirming this, Fire Chief got to his feet, stretched his legs, and followed Peyote Woman outside to get the pail of water used in the ritual. By now he knew the routine well enough.

Road Chief would sing a song of purification, followed by prayers from the other three officials. Next, water would be poured on the ground, the drum, and the altar. Only then would the holy water be passed around the circle for them to sip. They were supposed to take just enough to ease their dry throats, but he always took more. The next chance to get a drink would be at sunrise during the Morning Water Ceremony that concluded the official part of the meeting.

While they waited, they heard unexpected footsteps approaching the teepee, followed by a loud, angry voice. Had an intruder come to disrupt the meeting? Before any of them had time to react, Fire Chief came stumbling through the opening in the teepee and fell on top of his pail, spilling water on the fire. Steam hissed from the wet coals.

"What is it?" Road Chief glanced angrily from Fire Chief to the open canvas flap.

Suddenly a man with the head of a wolf stepped out of the darkness into the teepee.

Cedar Chief screamed at the sight of the wolf mask, with its rows of white teeth, its red tongue and snarling mouth.

The wolfman scanned the frightened faces, his small dark eyes peering out of twin openings in the mask, then raised his arm and pointed a long bony finger directly at him.

For a moment he felt paralyzed by fear. The mask looked like the head of a real wolf. Instinctively, he grabbed a handful of sand and tossed it at the intruder's eyes. Then he jumped to his feet and pushed past the wolfman outside where he stumbled into the woodpile and fell heavily to his knees. A burst of adrenaline gave him energy and cleared his mind. Ignoring the pain in his legs, he struggled to his feet and took off running across the desert. His car was parked about a hundred yards away, over near José Padilla's house. The shortest route would take him across a flat, open stretch of chamisa and piñon. That wouldn't do, too much visibility there.

Instead, he ran toward the deep arroyo offering protection that circled around behind Padilla's house. He could walk along the sandy bottom out of sight until he came to within twenty or thirty yards from his car. When he was sure the coast was clear, he could make a dash for it and get out of this place, Jacoñita. Away from the man with the wolf mask, whoever he was.

Finding the arroyo turned out to be easier than he expected once his eyes adjusted to the light of the half moon. He plunged down the steep bank and fell forward, sprawling on the cool sand. He paused a few moments to listen for the wolfman. Not a sound, so he scrambled to his feet and crept along the soft floor of the arroyo, being careful to avoid rocks. Several minutes later he took a look around, then climbed to the top of the arroyo and glanced back toward the teepee.

What he saw startled him. The fire inside the teepee illuminated the translucent white canvas from within, creating an eerie lantern effect. He could see shadows of the people inside, silhouetted against the glowing white canvas. The sight puzzled him. Why had the others stayed in the teepee? Where had the wolfman gone?

Something seemed wrong. He wondered if he was being double-crossed. Maybe Road Chief wanted the business all to himself. The bastard. He'd never trusted Reno. Not wanting to waste any more time, he walked faster, hurrying to get to his car. To the east he could see the distant lights of Santa Fe about twenty miles away. Much closer loomed the imposing mass of Black Mesa.

When the arroyo turned south, he knew he was getting close to where he needed to be. Close enough. He clawed his way up the crumbling bank and looked over the top at Padilla's house. Moonlight reflected off the dark windows and the pitched tin roof of the old adobe. He saw the square shape of Road Chief's van parked in the gravel lot beside the house. Then his black Porsche, no more than a hundred feet away, just beyond a patch of chamisa. An easy run.

He pulled himself out of the arroyo and, crouching low, moved out into the open. Moonlight and shadow, with strange noises everywhere. He heard the sound of small animals, probably lizards, scurrying under the bushes. From over near Black Mesa came a plaintive howl—a lone coyote.

His footsteps grew louder as he picked up speed. Finally he didn't care. He ran the last few yards, crashing through a tangle of chamisa, the branches ripping his shirt and scratching his bare arms. When he opened the door and dropped into the driver's seat, he found himself gasping for air. But he didn't stop to get his breath. He slammed the door and started the engine. Then he reached for the gearshift.

"Turn off the engine," came a deep voice from the back seat.

He gasped, his hand freezing in mid-air. In the rearview mirror was the face of a wolf.

There was just enough light to see white fangs and a red tongue hanging obscenely from the snarling, ghastly mask.

Part One: Fernando Lopez

1

Detective Fernando Lopez wished he'd had more time to put on his game face this morning. He didn't wake up so easily these days, not without his two cups of coffee. Age had begun to drain his energy and stiffen his joints. Hardly fitting for a patriarch, a man of honor from one of Santa Fe's oldest families.

He opened his 7-Eleven bag and took out the cup of steaming black coffee. He fumbled with the soggy containers of cream and sugar, dumped a little of each into cup and stirred the mixture with a No. 2 pencil courtesy of the Santa Fe Police Department. The taste of freshly brewed coffee jolted his senses. What he really needed this morning was a cigarette, but since he had quit smoking, more or less, he would have to make due with only coffee. He still kept an open pack of Camel Lights with him at all times, just to remind himself that he had the willpower to stop. And in case of an emergency.

From experience he knew he would be totally out of sorts until he had ingested the right amount of caffeine. He always seemed to be in a bad mood first thing Monday morning, but he was in an especially bad mood today because these two Indians were waiting for him when he walked into his office at half past eight. He hated not having time to put on his game face before all the people with problems began arriving.

He crumpled the 7-Eleven bag and tossed it on his desk with the Sonic Drive-In cups and the Great Burrito Company wrappers.

He took a sip of coffee. "What pueblo did you say you were from?"

"Zuni," replied the older man who'd introduced himself as Robert Naranjo and his friend as Billy Suino. He had a big belly and long black braids.

He frowned. He didn't see many Zunis. The Zuni Pueblo bordered Arizona, two hundred miles southwest of Santa Fe. Zunis usually took their problems to the Tribal Police or to the Gallup Police.

"We came to you because of this." The younger man took a folded piece of paper out of his shirt pocket and handed it to Fernando. He was wearing a Los Angeles Dodgers baseball cap pulled down over his forehead and a Nike T-shirt. He looked like the athletic type, slender and muscular, maybe a long distance runner.

He unfolded the paper which turned out to be a short letter addressed to the Zuni Tribal Council. The letter read: "If you want your ahayu:da back, go see Michael Soto, the owner of Sabado Indian Arts gallery in Santa Fe. Soto is trying to sell the ahayu:da around town for $50,000." The letter was signed: "A friend."

He read the letter again. It was typed. Cheap paper. Anonymous.

"Would you care to explain?"

The younger man looked angry. "Explain what? We want our ahayu:da back. That's why we're here."

He pronounced the Zuni word: ah – ha – yoo – dah.

Then Suino folded his arms across his chest, as though demanding immediate satisfaction. Wouldn't it be nice if things were that simple?

Sighing, he glanced at the ugly brown wall behind Suino, surveying his many plaques and awards from the Hispano Chamber of Commerce and the Fraternal Order of Police. His eyes came to rest on his citation framed in silver from the governor of New Mexico commemorating thirty long years of distinguished service to the city of Santa Fe.

Indians made him nervous, even after all these years as a cop. He preferred the term "Indians" to the politically correct "Native Americans." The fact that his ancestors had intermarried with both Indians and Anglos didn't make much difference. He couldn't help feeling they held him personally responsible for the Spanish conquest of New Mexico. The Spanish referred to it as the "Colonization," but the Indians called it theft, beginning with Coronado in 1540 and culminating in the government of Don

Juan de Oñate, the first official governor of the province known as "Nuevo Mexico." Over four hundred years had passed since Oñate arrived in 1598, but the Indians hadn't forgotten. Nor had they forgiven.

That was the problem with Santa Fe—too much history. People still held grudges about events that happened hundreds of years ago. Take Don Diego de Vargas and the Reconquest of New Mexico in 1692, twelve years after the northern pueblos had united forces and driven the Spanish settlers, soldiers, and priests, south to El Paso. The Pueblo Indians hated de Vargas and resented the Reconquest as much as or more than the original Colonization.

Was de Vargas a savior or a mass murderer? The answer depended on your point of view. Four hundred years hadn't eased tensions one bit. And the arrival of the Anglos in the 1800s had just added another layer of grudges.

"I'm sorry, but what's an ahayu:da?" he asked, hating to admit his ignorance. He wondered what Suino really wanted back. His land? The last four hundred years?

"A sacred war god. One of them was stolen this summer."

He squinted over the top of his coffee cup. "When you say 'sacred war god', what exactly do you mean? An object? A person? A spirit?"

Suino looked offended. He sat erect in the chair, his head held high. He was young and handsome with a long, thin nose and high cheekbones. "No, a carved wooden figure. A sacred carved wooden figure."

"So then, we're talking about an object," he said, reaching for a notepad.

Suino shrugged, not acknowledging his distinction.

"Here, take a look," the older man said, taking a cell phone out of his back pocket and showing him a photo. "See, our Deer and Bear Clans carve the ahayu:da," he added, nodding his head, trying to ease the tension between him and Suino. "We place them in sacred shrines on Zuni land. You know, leave them out in the open until they disintegrate. Because when they disintegrate, they replenish the earth."

He wrote all this down on a legal pad.

Naranjo continued. "Problem is, the ahayu:da can be

mischievous gods. They cause mischief if removed and not returned to their rightful places on the reservation."

"What kind of mischief?"

"Natural disasters, mostly. Earthquakes and floods. Like that."

He frowned. "Natural disasters?"

Naranjo nodded. "Unless returned to their shrines."

"You said someone stole an ahayu:da this summer. Do you have any idea who?'

"Could be anybody." Naranjo shook his round, weathered face. "An art dealer...a grave-robber...one of the hippies who come to hike on our land without asking permission. We see them all the time. We tell them to leave, but they just come back."

"Even a Zuni," Suino added. "One who's become greedy like an Anglo. Or a Mexican."

He knew Indians commonly referred to Hispanics as Mexicans, but common or not, he didn't like to be called a Mexican. Nor did he like this Suino fellow. Still, he had a job to do, so he tried to put aside his feelings and assume an air of polite informality. "Can these carvings be sold for as much as fifty thousand dollars?"

Suino shrugged. "How would we know, we don't sell our own ahayu:da."

He scratched his head. "Okay. Why don't you give me a description of the missing ahayu:da."

Suino corrected him. "Stolen."

He started to respond, then thought twice about it and took a drink of coffee instead.

Again Naranjo intervened. "It's slender, about thirty inches long, with a face carved in the wood."

He recorded the information. Then he passed the notepad to Naranjo. "Write down a phone number where I can reach you. Are you staying in town?"

"We thought maybe you could get the ahayu:da back today," Naranjo said.

He shook his head in disbelief. They didn't expect much, did they? "That depends. I'll talk to Soto, but I can't promise anything. For all I know, he might have already sold the ahayu:da. Or the letter might be a hoax. I'll get in touch with you as soon as I can."

"Then we'll stay in town," Suino said.

He didn't like the way Suino said that. It sounded like a threat. "Suit yourself."

Suino sprang to his feet and pulled the baseball cap lower on his forehead. Naranjo nodded, sighing as he got to his feet. He gave him an apologetic look, and then turned and followed his young companion into the dimly lit corridor outside his office.

Relieved to be alone, he settled back in his chair to relax. His mind began to clear, a process that seemed to take longer the older he got. Lately he'd been thinking about retiring. His wife wanted him to. His daughters, too.

They'd also convinced him to stop smoking. He finally gave in to their complaints and surprised them this past spring. They didn't know he still carried around his emergency pack of Camel Lights. What had his wife said last night? Something about his face being as wrinkled as a saguaro cactus. She blamed smoking for all his troubles, including the wrinkles, but he wasn't so sure.

Who wouldn't have wrinkles after thirty years of police work? Too many people with bad attitudes. That was a fact.

He didn't look forward to questioning Soto. Rich gallery owners were some of his least favorite people. He didn't know much about Soto, just that he'd bought Sabado Indian Arts on the Plaza. He'd seen Soto only once, at some function at City Hall. He couldn't remember the occasion, but he did remember the small man in the linen suit, very outgoing, a natural salesman. With his short black hair slicked back, Soto looked like a gigolo from a 1930s Hollywood movie. Hard to forget.

He took the opportunity to step outside for a breath of fresh air, just to clear his head. When he returned, he decided he needed another cup of coffee before making any decisions about how to proceed with this ahayu:da business, so he went down the hall to the coffee machine. He didn't like to drink coffee that came from a concession machine, but at the moment he didn't want to walk down the street to the Great Burrito Company.

From the hallway he spotted Fidel Rodriguez talking to the police dispatcher at the front counter. Sure as the sun rose every morning, Fidel or one of the other metro reporters from the *Santa*

Fe Independent would show up at the station about eight o'clock to read the police log for the latest criminal activity in the area. They loved the juicy stories, the murder and mayhem stuff. Fidel was one of the few reporters he admired because Fidel didn't sensationalize.

Fidel had manners. That was more than he could say for most of the hotshots who worked for the *Independent*.

"Fidel." He held up his cup.

"Are you buying?" Fidel, a small dapper man wearing a blue work shirt and red paisley tie, minus the jacket, asked.

"Sure, if you can drink this shit," he grumbled.

Fidel stuffed a notebook in his back pocket and stepped behind the counter.

He inserted more quarters in the coffee machine and handed Fidel a small paper cup filled with murky black liquid. "Santa Fe Concessions." He shook his head. "I think they're trying to poison us."

"Doing a pretty good job, too. You look like hell."

"Yeah, that's what my wife says. She tells me I'm smoking too much."

"I thought you quit."

"I did, sort of."

Fidel laughed. "So what do you have for me this morning? Any road kill last night?"

"Road kill? I hate that expression."

"Sorry, *cabrón*. Just a little humor."

While they talked, the police dispatcher answered a telephone call at the front desk. Linda Stephens jotted down the information and then turned to him. "Hey, Fernando, this must be your lucky day."

He liked Linda, a leftover hippie from the 1970s who'd managed to preserve her sardonic sense of humor. He saw her peering over the counter at him, steel-gray Afro, thick glasses, and a big smile on her face. From years of experience he knew what her smile meant—big trouble.

"Yeah?" he asked tentatively, not really wanting to know.

"Guy by the name of José Padilla just called to report a homicide in Jacoñita." Linda pushed the glasses back on her nose.

"Jacoñita? Where's Jacoñita?"

"You know, out by San Ildefonso Pueblo."

He nodded, remembering.

"Guess who our lucky victim is?"

Expecting the worst, he wasn't disappointed when he heard Linda say, "Michael Soto."

2

He shaded his eyes from the glare of the sunlight striking the tin roof of José Padilla's house and wished he hadn't forgotten his sunglasses. Just last week his wife had bought him an expensive pair that were supposed to block out 99.9 percent of all harmful rays. Estelle liked to warn him about cataracts, caused by too much sun coming through the deteriorating ozone layer. Leave it to his wife to always find something new to worry about.

Not surprisingly, Tomas Trujillo hadn't forgotten his sunglasses. The Ray-Bans were an essential part of his look, as were the short-sleeve shirts rolled up even shorter to reveal the bulging muscles left over from his days as a linebacker on the Santa Fe High School football team that won the state championship a few years back. He didn't care much for Trujillo—a deputy sheriff from Santa Fe Country—for the simple reason that Trujillo could never stop playing the tough guy. Trujillo had a short fuse and was always getting into trouble with his superiors for slapping people around. One of these days he would slap the wrong person and get his ass suspended.

He patted the pack of Camel Lights in his shirt pocket, always there if he needed them, while he listened to Trujillo and Padilla argue over by the crumbling adobe wall near the house. Padilla was a lousy liar, no doubt about it. He claimed not to have discovered Soto's body until eight this morning, a few minutes before calling 911. That story wasn't going to wash with anyone, because Soto had been dead at least eight hours by the time he and the lab technicians arrived.

The Porsche, with Soto's body inside, had been parked all night in Padilla's yard, no more than thirty feet from his front door. Not even a jury of his Hispanic peers would believe Padilla slept that soundly.

"Don't give me that bullshit," Trujillo said. "What happened last night? Why did you wait until this morning to call us?"

"I told you." Padilla nervously glanced from Trujillo to Fidel, who was listening to their conversation and scribbling notes in his small reporter's notebook.

"I noticed the car when I came out this morning. I was on my way to Santa Fe to buy groceries, and when I opened my gate—"

Trujillo stopped Padilla before he could finish the sentence. "Come on, you're not dressed to go shopping."

True, he thought. Padilla didn't look all that presentable, wearing filthy white painter's pants and a soiled blue denim work shirt. Not much of a looker anyway, with his wrinkled fifty-something face, he hadn't helped his appearance any by not shaving or combing his hair. He reeked of smoke, as if he'd just returned from a camping trip. The nights weren't cold enough for a fireplace or a wood burning stove.

Trujillo tried again. "What was Soto doing here last night?"

"Please," Padilla pleaded. "I told you. I found him this morning."

"Then what was Soto doing here this morning?"

Padilla looked at Fidel, as if searching for a friend.

"He came to buy something."

"Like what?"

"He wanted to buy an old Hopi kachina I was selling. For his gallery."

Trujillo persisted. "Why were you selling it?"

Padilla shrugged. "Because I needed the money."

He turned away, letting their voices blend together.

Let Trujillo take care of the interrogation. He didn't care, because it gave him more time to look around. He walked over to the shiny black Porsche, looking for something he'd missed earlier. Soto's body had been slumped against the steering wheel when he and Fidel had arrived. The hole in the back of Soto's head looked like the work of a small caliber bullet, maybe even a .22 fired at point-blank range. Soto was dressed casually, jeans and striped polo shirt, not the usual suits he wore around town playing the dandy.

Now that forensics had taken the body away, he could start his own investigation. Whoever killed Soto had been looking for something, that much was clear. How else to explain why the contents of the Porsche's trunk had been tossed haphazardly on the ground? He found a duffel bag ripped open with such force that its zipper had torn loose from the leather. Someone had taken everything out of the bag—a freshly laundered shirt, a pair of chinos, and a black leather shaving kit.

There were other items scattered about the parking lot including a first aid kit and a small Navajo rug. He also found tourists brochures from Taos and Acoma pueblos, an AAA envelope stuffed with road maps, and a white cotton bag empty except for a fine brown dust that he couldn't identify.

Had the killer found what he was looking for? Maybe, maybe not. He lowered his head and climbed into the passenger's seat. Sitting in a Porsche was a new experience for him. He drove a Plymouth and had never, even in his youth, owned anything more exotic than a Ford Mustang.

Well, he had news for Soto and all the other yuppies. The Porsche was too goddamned small. Why pay ninety thousand dollars or more for a car that was too goddamned small? Soto might be able to answer that, but Soto was dead.

He studied the car. He thought he smelled smoke. Definitely a hint, a faint trace of wood smoke. It was enough to make him wonder if Soto and Padilla had been camping last night. It was a crazy idea, but at the moment he had little else to work with. The interior of the car was clean except for coagulated blood on the driver's seat and the floor mat below. No apparent clues to what had happened last night. Opening the glove compartment, he found a flashlight and a map entitled "Guide to Indian Country," published by the Automobile Club of Southern California.

He unfolded the map, which delineated, in great detail and color, the various Indian reservations in the Four Corners area, including parts of Utah, Colorado, New Mexico, and Arizona.

Someone had taken a black felt-tip pen and traced along Highway 53, the back road to Zuni. The black marker followed

Highway 53 as it dipped down from Grants, skirted the El Malpais lava flow, passed through El Morro National Monument, and then followed the Rio Pescado into Zuni. He found one other black mark on the map—a circle drawn around the tiny town of Whitewater, a few miles north of Zuni on the highway to Gallup.

He refolded the map and stuffed it in his back pocket.

Before getting out, he checked the pool of blood under the driver's seat and noticed a few grains of fine white sand on the floor mat. Sand that fine and that white would have to come from the bottom of an arroyo. He climbed out of the car and looked around. He spotted an arroyo that began somewhere behind Padilla's house and circled around to the west toward Black Mesa. It was worth a try. He stepped between two dusty green chamisa bushes just beginning to flower and walked over to the arroyo. Not surprised, he saw a scattering of footprints in the sand. There was no way to tell how fresh the tracks were.

He heard footsteps behind him.

"Wait up."

He squinted into the sun, waiting for Fidel to join him.

"What do you think? Is Padilla lying?"

"Of course he's lying. You think he wouldn't notice a Porsche with a dead man inside parked all night in his front yard?"

Fidel nodded.

"Where does this arroyo go?" he mumbled, mostly to himself. He turned and walked along the edge of the arroyo, looking for some sign of recent activity, something. Fidel followed a few steps behind, careful to keep his distance.

Up ahead he saw Black Mesa rising from the desert floor, a slab of black rock silhouetted against the blue New Mexico sky.

He carefully made his way over the rough terrain, avoiding patches of cholla and prickly pear cactus while following the twists and turns of the arroyo. He noticed an abundance of animal tracks, dogs or coyotes, as he moved farther away from Padilla's house. Then he noticed something else. Part of the bank had crumbled, as if someone had fallen over the edge. Loose rocks had collected at the bottom of the arroyo, near a place where the soft sand had been recently upturned. He thought he saw handprints.

He followed an imaginary line that began at the point of

the handprints, passed through the spot where the bank had crumbled, and extended out indefinitely in the general direction from which someone running for his life would have come before stumbling into the arroyo. Soto, perhaps.

"Help me out. My eyes aren't as good as they used to be. What do you see over there?"

Fidel looked in the direction he pointed. He studied the desert terrain. "Is that an old campfire?"

"Where?"

"Right there, to the left of the piñon trees," Fidel answered.

He walked quickly toward the trees. He, too, spotted the remains of a campfire. A thin wisp of smoke coiled like a ghost over the black embers. As he approached he realized someone had poured water on the fire not long ago. He kicked at the charred pieces of wood that remained, watching the coals underneath begin to spark and recognized the scent of piñon wood.

It was the same smell he'd noticed on Padilla and in the front seat of Soto's Porsche.

"Look at this," Fidel said, pointing to a series of indentations in the sandy earth. The indentations were round, about four inches in diameter, and together formed a circle around the fire. The campfire had been located near the center of the circle. To be exact, the campfire had been located near the center of a teepee, which meant that someone had been camping here or holding some kind of ceremony. New Mexico was overrun with New Age types who were always going out in the desert for retreats and ceremonies of one kind or another, New Age religions or practices that he didn't understand. He hoped it was that, not what he feared.

He squatted down on his haunches to get a better look. Near the fire someone had drawn, then later partially erased, a half circle in the sand.

He dug in the soft sand, carefully scraping away one layer at a time. He quickly found what he was looking for. What he hoped he wouldn't find.

"Peyote," Fidel said, when he held up the small brown button about the size of a quarter.

He nodded. "Soto came out here last night to attend a peyote ceremony."

Fidel looked at him. "Native American Church?"

"Maybe." He dropped the peyote button in his shirt pocket. "Give me a hand here."

Fidel helped him up.

He took a bandana out of his back pocket and wiped his damp forehead. He was already sweating and the day was still young.

Overhead the sun scorched the blue sky, unusually hot for late August. He looked back at Padilla's house and wished he'd remembered to wear his new sunglasses. Beginning to worry, he thought he could feel his eyes fogging up with cataracts. Soon he'd be blind. Then Estelle would say, "I told you so." He'd have no one to blame but himself.

"So Padilla belongs to the Native American Church," Fidel said, after a long pause.

He turned, remembering Fidel. "That's why he didn't report Soto's body until this morning—to give them time to pack up the teepee and get the hell out of here."

"Why would they want to conceal the meeting? The Native American Church is legal—"

He was interrupted by the sound of a distant "crack" and then the zing of a bullet kicking up sand just to their right in the direction of the arroyo.

"Get down!" he yelled, as the two dived into the sand.

Just then a second bullet struck behind them, closer to the house.

Fidel tried to get up.

"Wait!" He grabbed Fidel around the waist and pulled him back down. "Just listen."

They heard nothing. Just silence. After about a minute, he rose to his knees slowly, looking around at the distant mesas over toward the Rio Grande. He saw no obvious places where a shooter could be situated. The shot was from a high-powered rifle, fired from a great distance. He could tell by the sound.

"Shit," Fidel said. "I didn't sign up for this, I'm a fucking news reporter."

He ignored Fidel, standing up now and looking around for any possible movement on the mesas, a shooter, a vehicle, something.

"Where did it come from?"

He pointed toward the river. "Whoever it was, he's probably gone now."

"Yeah, well I'm getting the hell out of here." Crouching low, Fidel scurried off into the sagebrush like a human crab, heading toward Padilla's house.

He made a mental note to send someone out later to try and find one of the bullets. Good luck with that.

He frowned. The day was shaping up even worse than he expected. Getting involved with the Native American Church, or some renegade branch of the church, was the last thing he wanted to do.

Technically, Fidel spoke correctly. The courts had ruled that peyote ceremonies were legal if held as official meetings of the church. The legal issue didn't bother him. Never had.

But having to deal with trigger-happy members of the church did bother him. They were the kind of people who gathered in teepees at night to gobble peyote, a hallucinogenic drug similar to LSD that induced visions of...what? The world of spirits and apparitions? He didn't even know what to call it, never being one to believe in a spirit world. He was just trying to make sense of the one he inhabited, the physical world. Just thinking about the Native American Church gave him a headache.

He heard Trujillo's loud, angry voice coming from inside the small adobe as he approached. He hurried inside, hoping he wouldn't be too late to stop the rough stuff.

Fearing the worst, he breathed a sigh of relief when he found Padilla unharmed. The disheveled little man stood in one corner of his living room where he seemed to be showing Trujillo a finely carved kachina on the mantle above his fireplace. The kachina stood about eighteen inches tall, but brown and gold eagle feathers on its headdress made it appear much taller. The brightly-colored kachina danced in full costume, with a red cloth sash tied around its yellow waist, waving a gourd rattle in its right hand.

“Soto offered me five thousand dollars,” Padilla said. “It’s probably worth a lot more, because it’s a Hemis kachina carved in the nineteen twenties.”

He walked to the fireplace, negotiating a maze of worn sofas and stuffed chairs faded to a dull beige color. The other two men made room for him.

“When was Soto going to buy the kachina?” he asked suddenly. “Before or after the peyote ceremony?”

Padilla’s jaw tightened.

He could see the tension in Padilla’s face.

Trujillo looked puzzled, as if he’d missed something.

“I can’t talk about the church. Our ceremonies are secret. It’s a question of religious freedom.”

“Not when murder’s involved, it’s not,” he said, raising his voice.

Trujillo moved closer to Padilla, who shrank back against the whitewashed adobe wall.

“Now...I want you to tell me the names of everyone who came to the meeting last night. Then I want you to tell me exactly what happened. Everything from sunset to sunrise.”

3

Arms folded across his chest, he sat at his desk studying the peyote button he'd found at Jacoñita. The button looked harmless enough—brown, wrinkled, and no larger than a dried apricot. He knew peyote came from a small, blue cactus that grew wild in parts of southern Texas and Mexico. The cactus produced white flowers, as well as mushroom-like crowns that contained mescaline, a naturally occurring psychedelic drug that produced vivid hallucinations and deep introspection and finally nausea. Members of the Native American Church prized the dried crowns and used them in their all-night meetings. When chewed during the meetings, peyote induced extraordinary physiological and psychological effects such as visions, bright colors, and dramatic changes in time and perception. Some people argued that peyote unlocked the door to a separate, higher reality.

He knew peyote could be a potent drug, because he'd made the mistake of eating a couple of buttons one fourth of July afternoon at Cañjilon Lakes. It seemed like a million years ago—1968, or maybe 1969. The Lopez family—including an assortment of aunts, uncles, and cousins—had gone up to Cañjilon for a weekend of camping and fishing. His cousin Manuel, who was a member of the Native American Church, brought a bag of peyote and shared it with him and some of the older cousins. He could still remember wandering off by himself to lie in the grass and watch the sky change colors like a giant kaleidoscope. He didn't remember how long he laid there, only the feeling of being incapacitated, unable to move.

Personally, he didn't care much for the feeling, or for the

sense of powerlessness he experienced while under the influence of the drug. The loss of control frightened him.

Manuel made fun of him. Called him a "tight ass" and lectured him on the importance of seeing beyond one's individuality. Individuality was a prison, Manuel said.

Maybe so, but he wasn't comfortable with the loss of control. That's the way he'd always been. Manuel could go fuck himself if he didn't like it. Which is what he had told him back in 1968. Whenever it was.

The Indians were different, of course. He had no problem with Indians using peyote. He knew the Navajo and Pueblo Indians had used peyote in religious ceremonies for hundreds of years before the Spanish arrived. Predictably, the Spanish tried to stop the practice by persuasion and, when that failed, force. No doubt about it, the Spanish had been heavy-handed in their efforts to stamp out the "pagan" religions of the indigenous peoples, issuing decrees that prohibited religious dances and other ceremonies, and destroying whatever religious masks and icons their searches uncovered at the various pueblos. Talk about stupidity. It always amazed him that people could be so lacking in judgment.

He did not consider himself religious, a fact that distressed Estelle, but even he recognized that the sword was not an effective means of religious conversion. Times had changed, or so his wife argued whenever they discussed this murky subject. But had they really, given the never-ending ethnic cleansing and sectarian violence that still plagued the world? He could trace his family's presence in New Mexico back to 1630, the year Salvador de Lopez, originally of Valladolid, Spain, came to Santa Fe. A soldier and a blacksmith by trade, Salvador accompanied a mission supply train up the El Camino Real trail from Mexico City to Santa Fe.

He took pride in his family's history and in the Spanish contribution to the cultural mix of New Mexico. Still, certain things bothered him, especially the religious persecution of the Indians. Today, most Hispanics chose not to remember that their ancestors brought the Inquisition to New Mexico. In 1625 friars acting as agents on behalf of the Holy Office of the Inquisition set up shop at Santo Domingo Pueblo south of Santa Fe. Some of the earliest Inquisition documents surviving at Santo Domingo concerned the "crime" of peyote use among the Pueblo Indians.

Shaking his head, he took the peyote button, protected by a plastic bag, and deposited it safely in his desk.

Already he saw some progress in the investigation. Padilla now acknowledged that Soto had died last night during the peyote ceremony. No big surprise there. By Padilla's count eight people had attended the meeting—Sammy Tso and Dora Alvarez from San Ildefonso Pueblo, the five officers who conducted the ceremony, and Soto. While Padilla admitted to serving as Fire Chief, he denied knowing the identities of the other officers, only that the four of them—three men and one woman—lived somewhere near Gallup.

Just where in Gallup, Padilla refused to say. He claimed Soto had organized the meeting and that the other officers were friends of Soto's.

So much bullshit, that last part. But he had to give Padilla credit. He proved to be a tough nut to crack. Not even Trujillo's crude attempts at intimidation had broken him.

Once again he read Padilla's statement:

"The meeting ended about midnight, just before Midnight Water Call. Peyote Woman and I stepped outside the teepee to get a pail of water. She came along to bless the water, but it was my responsibility as Fire Chief to bring it inside. When I turned to go back in the teepee, I heard footsteps coming up behind me. That's when I saw him, the wolfman. He was wearing a wolf mask, with big white fangs and red tongue. I screamed at him to go away and leave us alone.

"'Get out of my way!' he shouted, then shoved me through the door of the teepee. The water spilled, and I fell on top of the pail. When I looked up, Michael Soto and the wolfman ran out of the teepee. Everyone was scared. We waited inside the teepee for about ten minutes, until we heard a gunshot. Then Road Chief went out to see what had happened. When he came back, he told us Michael Soto had been shot dead.

"Dora Alvarez started screaming and wouldn't stop, so Sammy Tso took her home, back to San Ildefonso. Road Chief said a prayer to call off the meeting, and then we took down the teepee and the poles and loaded them on top of Road Chief's van. The four of them left before sunrise, about an hour before I called you. That's it, that's everything that happened."

Great. A werewolf was all he needed to make the day complete.

He tossed the paper back on his cluttered desk. He didn't know what to make of the wolfman. Maybe Padilla had eaten too much peyote, so much that he'd experienced visions of ghosts and spirits and men turning into wolves under the light of a full moon. Or maybe, more likely, it was someone wearing a wolf mask. Someone who wanted Soto dead.

He checked the time. Nearly two p.m. Padilla had been waiting in the back room with Sergeant Antonio Blake for two hours now. They would have to release him soon enough, but Padilla didn't know that. He hoped the wait with Antonio, a former Marine with notoriously gruff manners, would help refresh Padilla's memory. Spending time with Antonio was like getting a dose of truth serum.

Finally he picked up the telephone. "Antonio, bring Padilla to my office." He wanted to ask Padilla a few more questions before releasing him.

Antonio escorted Padilla into the office, then folded his arms and waited for instructions. An angry glare was fixed on the stocky ex-Marine's face.

He noticed the change immediately. Padilla looked unsure of himself, nervous.

"Sit down." He motioned to the gray metal chairs where Naranjo and Suino had sat a few hours earlier.

Padilla did as he was told.

He waved to Antonio, who disappeared down the corridor.

"First, I want to know more about Road Chief and the other officers. Who are these people? Do they usually travel together to the peyote meetings?"

"All I know is that Road Chief and his wife were friends of Soto's." Padilla sighed, tired of answering the same questions.

He raised his eyebrows. "Road Chief's wife? Peyote Woman?"

"Right. They live out near Gallup. So do the others, I think. Like I told you before, Soto arranged the peyote meeting himself.

He wanted to hold it near San Ildefonso, so I let him use my land. Soto did the rest."

"But you served as Fire Chief."

Padilla shrugged. "It's common for the host to act as Fire Chief. Fire Chief watches the door of the teepee, brings in wood and tends the fire, things like that."

"Was Road Chief a Zuni? Were any of the officers Zuni?"

"Zuni?" Padilla looked puzzled. "Road Chief's an Anglo. So's Drummer Chief and Cedar Chief. Peyote Woman might be Zuni. Some kind of Indian."

He gave Padilla a legal pad. "Write down descriptions of them. Everything you can remember."

He walked to the window and looked out through the Venetian blinds at the municipal parking lot that separated the police station from the new Santa Fe Public Library. He could still remember when the library was across the street, before some silly developer with the backing of City Council came up with the bright idea to build a pueblo-style mall called the First Interstate where the old library stood.

"Okay." He walked back to his desk. "Now tell me this. Why did Soto want to hold the peyote meeting near San Ildefonso?"

Padilla blushed. "Well...he was looking for business."

"Business? What kind of business?"

"For his gallery. It was like I told you before. He was going to buy my Hopi kachina. And I'd sold him other things, a couple of santos and a buffalo dancer kachina. So had Dora Alvarez, I think. That's how Soto got a lot of the merchandise for his gallery. He bought it from people like Dora and me."

He frowned, not liking what he was hearing. "You mean Soto staged the peyote meetings? He used the Native American Church in order to locate tribal objects and family heirlooms to buy?"

Padilla shrugged.

"Is that how he stole the ahayu:da?"

Padilla stared blankly at him. "The what?"

"The ahayu:da. Did Soto steal that, too? Or did he buy it from someone who did?"

Padilla shook his head, either confused or pretending to be confused. He couldn't decide which.

"Some poor slob who had to sell his own tribal heritage for a few dollars?"

"So what?" Padilla shot back, raising his voice for the first time. "At least he paid for what he took."

He glared at Padilla, surprised at the little man's outburst.

Padilla no longer bothered containing his hostility. "Tell me, what else are we supposed to do? Sell fucking trinkets on the Plaza? We're just trying to stay alive, like everybody else. Look at you. You've sold out to the system, you and all the other cops. Who do you think pays your wages? You set yourself against the People."

"Yeah—fuck you, Padilla!" he snapped, having heard this bullshit before. "What people are you talking about? People like you? Thieves like you? Is that your definition of the People?" He fought hard to control his emotions.

"I'm leaving. If you want me, you know where to find me."

He watched Padilla walk swiftly out of the office. He was sick and tired of punks like Padilla telling him that he'd sold out to the system. Being accused of selling out was a sore spot with him. He'd heard it repeatedly over the years and was fucking tired of hearing it.

Feeling claustrophobic, he pulled up the Venetian blinds and opened the window to let in some fresh air.

The gentle breeze on his face lifted his spirits. He needed to get out of this cluttered old office that stank of coffee and cigarette smoke and thirty years of police work. He decided to walk over to the Great Burrito Company for a cup of coffee and maybe something to eat.

The telephone rang before he could leave.

"Fidel Rodriguez from the Independent on line two," Linda said from the front desk.

"Fernando, this is Fidel. I'm calling to find out if there's anything new in the Soto case."

Fernando sighed. "Nothing yet."

"Yeah?" Fidel sounded skeptical, as though insinuating he was withholding something.

"Listen, will you do me a favor?" He changed the subject.

"I need some background information. Do you know what an ahayu:da is?"

"You mean the Zuni war god?"

"Exactly. The Zuni carve the wooden figures and then place them in shrines on Zuni land. Sometimes the figures are stolen and end up in museums or private collections. Could you check your files at the *Independent* for any stories or photographs? Recent stories, especially."

"No problem. What are you looking for? Is there a connection between Soto's murder and a stolen ahayu:da?"

"Maybe. Two Zunis came to see me this morning. They think Soto was trying to sell an ahayu:da on the black market." He could hear Fidel scribbling notes at the other end of the line.

"I'll be over in a few minutes." He hung up quickly before Fidel could ask any more questions.

On his way out he winked at Linda.

She smiled and shook her head. "Don't start."

He walked down to the Great Burrito Company and ordered a cup of coffee to go, ignoring the tourists sitting at the outside tables. He took the coffee up Marcy Street to the office of the *Independent*. Only ten minutes had passed since he'd hung up the phone, but that ought to be enough time. If Fidel was as efficient as he suspected.

"*Bueñas Dias*," he said to Adellita, the receptionist, as he walked into the newsroom.

Adellita smiled, a young woman with streaks of red sprayed in her hair and tattoos on her bare arms. He didn't get it. Why would anyone want sprayed red hair? Or tattoos on their arms?

Fidel waved him over to his terminal. "We have one photo in our file. It's a reproduction of a nineteen twenty-five photograph taken by Edward S. Curtis. The original comes from the Museum of New Mexico Photo Archives. I'll give you the negative number and our librarian will make you a copy."

"Thanks." He spilled coffee on the carpet as he took a seat at the next terminal.

"The most recent story I can find dates from this past spring when an ahayu:da was stolen from its shrine near Thunder Mountain on the Zuni Reservation. As far as I know, it hasn't been recovered. Before that we go back two years, when an ahayu:da turned up in a Paris auction house. Paris, France. The Zuni took the auction house to court and argued that the bill of sale for the figure was invalid because sacred tribal objects were communal property and could not be sold by an individual. The case is still making its way through the courts."

"Nothing more recent?"

Fidel punched a few more keys at his terminal and then shook his head. "Wait, here's something else. Several years ago the Zuni successfully pressured the Smithsonian Museum to return an ahayu:da that had been part of the Frank H. Cushing Collection at the Smithsonian."

He squinted at the monitor, trying to read the screen. "The what?"

"The Frank H. Cushing Collection. You know, the ethnologist who lived at Zuni Pueblo in the eighteen eigthies."

While they talked, a young woman with long blond hair tied behind her head in a ponytail walked into the newsroom. "Here's a copy of the photo you wanted."

"Thanks, Anne."

Fernando scooted his chair closer. "So that's what an ahayu:da looks like. I'll be damned."

"See, there are actually two kinds, Big Brother and Little Brother."

He studied the black and white photograph that showed a pile of ahayu:da in varying stages of decomposition. Two of the carved figures stood erect, rising out of a small patch of dried grass and prickly pear cactus, a Big Brother in front and a Little Brother behind.

Just as Fidel said, the two figures were entirely different. Big Brother displayed an elongated, helmet-like face and what looked like a phallus sticking straight out from its middle. More abstract and unformed, Little Brother had no face or phallus, but instead a series of geometric shapes carved on its body—half moons, circles, and crosses.

Fidel laughed. "This is supposed to be an umbilical cord." He pointed to Big Brother. "In spite of what it looks like."

But he wasn't looking at Big Brother. He couldn't take his

eyes away from the symbols carved on Little Brother.

Where had he seen them before? Then he remembered. The very same symbols were drawn in the sand at Jacoñita, in the circle of the teepee.

4

He had never been inside Sabado Indian Arts on the Plaza, one of the newer galleries in Santa Fe. He found himself sitting in the back office with store manager Wanda LeClair, a small shapely woman with strawberry blond hair wearing a tight black dress that revealed every curve. Like Soto, she was drop dead gorgeous, one of the Beautiful People. Except they weren't so beautiful now. Soto was dead and she had been weeping nonstop since he'd delivered the news about her boss. To escape her blubbering, he walked into Soto's office and took a seat at the desk. Unfortunately, she followed him, bringing with her a box of tissues. She sat on the black leather sofa wiping her eyes with one tissue after another.

The sound of women crying made him uncomfortable. Something to do with male guilt, he supposed, though he didn't really care to explore the subterranean levels of the male psyche, his in particular. Too much self-knowledge could be a dangerous thing.

He knew very well that he should say something consoling to her, since he'd been the indirect agent of her grief, having delivered the bad news. Her decision to follow him into the office meant that she expected him to offer comfort of some sort. But what, precisely, could he say or do? Bring Soto back to life? If he could do that, he wouldn't be wasting his time working for the Santa Fe Police Department.

"I'm sorry," he said finally. It wasn't much, but enough to break the impasse.

She nodded and reached for another tissue. "I just can't believe it. Everyone loved Michael. He was such a nice guy."

"Not everyone."

She looked at him in horror, as though he'd uttered something disrespectful to the dead, something obscene.

Taken aback by her reaction, he fumbled for the right words. "What I mean is, Soto had at least one enemy. Can you think of anyone who might have had a reason to kill him? A dissatisfied customer, perhaps."

She shook her head and brushed the hair out of her eyes, no longer weeping.

"Or, let's say someone who wanted to get back a sacred tribal object...one that Soto might have been selling on the black market—an ahayu:da, for example?"

"What's that? You mean the Zuni War god? The carving?"

"Correct." He explained about the stolen ahayu:da and the letter Suino and Naranjo had shown him earlier.

She shook her head again. "I don't believe it. Michael wasn't the type to deal in black market art. Why would he? He made a lot of money selling legal Indian art."

He shrugged, not getting a read on this woman. Was she as innocent as she pretended? Or was she covering up her involvement in Soto's black market business?

"Well," he said finally. "We do know he pretended to be a member of the Native American Church in order to buy tribal objects from the people he met at peyote meetings."

"Michael may have gone to some peyote meetings to meet people, to make contact with craftspeople and clients, but he wasn't selling on the black market, I'm sure. I mean, I think I would have known if he was doing something illegal. We were very close."

"How close?"

"Close enough to know if he were selling stolen property."

Watching her performance, he began to wonder if she had been in love with Soto. Naturally all the women would fall for someone like Soto. He was handsome, slick, and obviously rich.

"Excuse me. I need to look around the office. If you don't mind."

Taking the hint, she stood up with her box of tissues. Then she turned and walked out.

He fidgeted at the desk. Soto's office was a study in black and white: black furniture, white walls. Even the expensive Navajo rugs hanging on the wall were woven of black and gray wool. The room needed some color, he decided. Surely, with a gallery filled with colorful Indian arts—rugs, pottery, and jewelry—Soto could have added a splash of color to the room. Even one of the kachinas behind the counter would have helped.

He went over to the emergency exit and threw open the back door, exposing the narrow brick alley. It contrasted sharply with the slick interior of Soto's office. He studied the crumbling brick and adobe walls, splotched with layers of mud stucco and covered with graffiti.

The patched, discolored walls, even the overturned trash cans in the alley cheered him slightly, though he couldn't say exactly why. The slogans spray-painted on the alley walls were as ugly here as they were elsewhere around the city. Throw open the door, look underneath the glitz, and what do you find? "Go back to Texas." "Fuck you, Anglo pigs!" Everywhere the same tensions, sometimes hidden, sometimes not.

He walked back to the desk and put up his feet, thinking. He'd already examined the contents of Soto's desk, including computer printouts listing each item in Sabado's inventory by number and description, date and price of purchase, and date and price of sale, if sold. None of the entries on these lists looked suspicious, which probably meant that Soto kept his black market activities off-list. The desk also contained a collection of business cards from art galleries in New Mexico and Arizona that Soto may have done business with. Odds and ends. No mention of the ahayu:da.

One thing he did find was a locked broom closet at the end of the hallway, which made him wonder why anyone would lock a broom closet. When he asked to open the door, the LeClair woman said she didn't have a key, that Soto kept the only key to the closet. That meant he would have to get a warrant and a locksmith to open the door one way or another. He could do all that tomorrow when he had more time and patience.

Still, the possibility that he might be overlooking something else, something obvious, kept him from leaving. He checked his watch. Still enough time to drive out to Hyde Park Estates, where

Soto had recently purchased a new condo, and make it home by six thirty.

His wife hated for him to be late for dinner, even after all these years of police work. Estelle had never gotten used to his irregular hours. For thirty years she'd stubbornly refused to reconcile herself to the unpredictable and often inconvenient disruptions of daily routine that came with his job.

Maybe non-acceptance was her form of acceptance. Did that make any sense?

While he considered what to do next, he heard voices coming from the front of the gallery. Wanda was explaining to someone that the gallery was closed for the day. "No, I'm sorry, but you'll have to leave," she said, raising her voice. Apparently her words had no effect, because the very next moment she shouted, "Wait! Where do you think you're going? Stop or I'll call the police."

Had she forgotten about him? He was, after all, the police.

He listened to the approaching footsteps. Loud, angry footsteps. Suddenly two men burst into the office, with Wanda following closely on their heels. The Los Angeles Dodgers baseball cap tipped him off even before he got a good look at the faces of Suino and Naranjo. Immediately his spirits sank. He would never make it home by six thirty now.

Estelle would not be happy tonight.

The two Indians paused momentarily when they saw him sitting with his feet up on the desk. Naranjo looked nervous, but not Suino. Suino began to search the office, as if he didn't exist. An invisible man.

"What the hell do you want?" He was not happy with this unwanted intrusion.

"I told them we were closed, but they wouldn't listen," Wanda said.

Suino ignored her. "What do you think we want? We're looking for our ahayu:da. We didn't find it in Soto's room at La Fonda, so now we've come to check his gallery."

He took his feet off the desk and sat up straight. "What are you talking about? Soto lives in Hyde Park Estates."

Suino looked at him blankly, a look of incredulity on his young face.

"Not exactly," Wanda interjected, embarrassed for him. "That's a mistake. The new directory lists his address as Hyde Park Estates, but his condo isn't quite finished, so he's living at La Fonda. Had been living at La Fonda."

Suino looked at him. "You didn't know that?"

He ignored the question. He stared at Suino for a few moments, then changed the subject. "I forget. Where did you say you were staying in Santa Fe?"

Naranjo answered, sucking in his big belly. "Tesuque Pueblo."

He smiled. By his calculation Tesuque Pueblo was less than ten miles from Jacoñita—logistically, an insignificant distance for a murderer bold enough to stalk his victim at a peyote ceremony. A wolfman, perhaps. Or someone pretending to be a wolfman.

"Both of you stayed at Tesuque Pueblo last night? Is that correct?"

Naranjo nodded.

"So what?" Suino wanted to know.

"I'll tell you so what." He stood up from the desk and walked toward Suino. "Someone murdered Michael Soto last night at Jacoñita, a few miles from Tesuque Pueblo."

"Yeah? Did Soto have the ahayu:da with him?"

'We don't know if he had the ahayu:da with him, but the person who killed him went through his car trying to find it. So tell me, were you in Jacoñita last night?"

"Then it's still missing."

"Answer my question!" he shouted.

"How can you find anything sitting around here?"

Losing control, he grabbed Suino by the T-shirt and slammed him back against the wall, cracking the plaster. He twisted the collar around Suino's neck, choking him.

Suino grabbed his hand and tried to push him away, but he slammed him back into the wall again. Plaster showered the floor.

The sudden violence surprised Wanda, who screamed and ran out of the office.

Naranjo pleaded with him. "Don't hurt him, please. He's just a smart-ass kid."

He felt the blood pounding through his veins, and he heard the muffled voice of Naranjo talking to him. It took a moment, but he managed to control his impulse to smash Suino's face. Finally he let go of the T-shirt, and then tried to smooth the twisted fabric by patting it against the man's chest.

It had been a long time since he'd lost his temper like that. He didn't like the feeling. He needed to do a better job of controlling his emotions.

Suino stared impassively at him, pure hatred in his eyes.

"Come with me—both of you. We're going back to La Fonda." He brushed past Wanda, who stood watching from the safety of the doorway, then marched across the wooden floor of the gallery. He heard Suino and Naranjo following along behind.

Walking the short distance to La Fonda didn't provide enough time for an attitude adjustment. When he stepped into the colorful Mexican-style lobby, hand painted tiles and potted palms, he found it almost as crowded as the Plaza. He heard mariachis playing in the bar and the murmur of a hundred voices talking at once. Oddly enough, he spotted the hulking figure of Antonio at the front desk, talking to Fred Mondragon, the manager.

Some sort of disturbance must have occurred, because Antonio was taking notes while Mondragon gestured toward a bellhop who stood between the two older men. What the hell now? He pushed his way through the crowd toward the blue uniform of Antonio who, at six feet seven inches tall, towered over Mondragon, the bellhop, and everyone else in the noisy lobby.

"What's the problem?"

Antonio shook his head. "Got a report here that two Indians were seen prowling around upstairs." He sounded annoyed, as if he thought the whole thing was a waste of his time.

"Not prowling," Mondragon protested, a neat little man wearing a tan suit and a necktie that was as white as his hair. "Jimmy saw them come out of one of the rooms. Go on, tell the man, Jimmy."

The bellhop started to say something, then stopped abruptly when he saw Suino and Naranjo coming up behind him. "There. That's them." He pointed at Suino and Naranjo. "The two men I saw leaving the room."

"Grab them!" Mondragon shouted.

But Suino was too fast. He shoved him hard in the back, sending him flying into a man wearing a backpack and then into a tall beanpole of a woman wearing a straw sombrero. Falling, he grabbed the woman around the waist and felt his nose press up against the heavy squash blossom that dangled between her breasts.

"Get off me!" the woman screamed, swatting him on the head with her purse. The blow knocked him sideways and sent him reeling to the floor, where he landed on his elbow. He gasped for air as a sharp pain shot up his right arm into his shoulder. By this time everyone in the lobby seemed to be pushing and shoving and shouting at one another.

He tried to make amends. "Sorry...sorry."

Amid the chaos, he struggled to a sitting position, fearful of being trampled by the mob of rowdy tourists. No way he could let that happen, he told himself, struggling to get to his feet. Luckily, the tall woman with the sombrero had been pushed back toward the bar where she staggered from side to side like a wounded animal, screaming and flailing away with her purse at anyone who came near enough for her to swat.

"Stop it!" Mondragon shouted, raising his arms. With the help of the bellhop, he climbed up on the front desk and looked down on the angry mob. "Please. Calm down. Stop pushing. There's been a misunderstanding. Please. Clear out and give us some room. Someone's been injured."

He realized that Mondragon meant him. He was the injured person.

Slowly the crowd began to disperse.

As the noise subsided, he could hear Antonio speaking to him.

"Are you okay? Fernando? Are you okay?"

"Yeah...sure...I think so." He let Antonio help him to his feet. He rubbed his sore arm and then glanced around the lobby.

"They're gone. They ran outside. Someone said they went up San Francisco Street past the cathedral."

He frowned. "I know where to find them." He turned to Mondragon. "Do you want to press charges?"

Mondragon shook his head. "Not really. Not if you can keep

them out of here. They didn't take anything, according to Jimmy. So why bother, unless they come back."

Both Antonio and the bellhop had to help Mondragon down from the front desk.

Leaving Antonio to make peace in the lobby, he got a key to Soto's room from the front desk and took the elevator to the fifth floor. As soon as he stepped out he lit his emergency cigarette, tossing the match on the terra-cotta tile floor. The burst of nicotine picked him up immediately, just enough to make him feel capable of taking care of this last piece of business. He bypassed the chance to rest a moment on the hand-carved bench in the sitting area across from the elevator. For a little while longer he would have to run on sheer determination.

Down the dark carpeted hallway—its walls lined with Mexican tiles and pressed-tin light fixtures—he found Soto's room and unlocked the door. The room turned out to be a small suite complete with sitting room, bedroom, and bath. There was even a balcony overlooking La Fonda's pool three floors below. The pool shocked him. He had no idea La Fonda had such amenities. Imagine that. Living in a city for sixty years and not knowing that its most famous downtown hotel had a swimming pool. What else didn't he know about Santa Fe?

"This is a non-smoking room," someone said from the hallway behind him.

He turned to find a skinny maid with chemically blond hair carrying a stack of clean towels.

"I'm a police detective." He showed her his badge.

She ignored the badge. "Did you know that John Kennedy stayed in this room when he came to Santa Fe in nineteen sixty?"

"No kidding. So Kennedy and Michael Soto have at least two things in common."

"Two things?" The maid looked puzzled, waiting for an explanation.

"If you will excuse me." He closed the door in her face.

Once again he could not locate an ashtray, so he tossed his cigarette in a potted cactus by the door. Then he crossed the room and stepped out on the balcony, which turned out to be a mistake because as soon as he did he spotted the tall woman with the sombrero sitting at a poolside table sipping a gigantic mixed drink. Even from this distance he could see the pink color of the murky concoction, complete with doll-size umbrellas. When the woman pointed him out to her companions, two other women wearing layers of turquoise jewelry, he frowned and went back into the room.

A horrible thought occurred to him. Maybe he would keep running into this woman. Forever.

Sitting on the Taos sofa, he surveyed the room. He couldn't help but admire the handcrafted furniture, all rubbed with the same gray wash and embellished with the some motifs, zigzag arrows, bear claws, and feather plumes. Not bad for five hundred dollars a day, or whatever Soto paid to live at La Fonda. The sitting room came equipped with a wet bar stocked with bottles of scotch, tequila, and exotic liqueurs. Not bad at all. He put his feet on the coffee table and looked around the room, impeccably arranged and decorated in the best Southwestern style. For people who could afford it.

People like Soto. And John Kennedy.

But for all the expensive Southwestern décor, the room still looked like a sterile hotel room. In contrast, the bedroom looked lived in. On the floor he found a pile of books, a plastic bag stuffed with soiled clothes, and a cardboard box containing Indian pots, individually wrapped in plastic foam.

He checked the two side-by-side trasteros that served as closets. Soto's collection of Giorgio Armani suits impressed him, as did the rows of silk and linen shirts. A real yuppie, all right. Too fancy for his taste. Then something caught his eye in the second trastero. A row of women's clothing. Dresses and an assortment of skirts and blouses. Interesting. Either Soto enjoyed cross-dressing, or he'd had a frequent overnight guest. Wanda LeClair?

After he finished rummaging through Soto's clothes, he decided to call it quits. He'd have to come back tomorrow when he had more time, and more energy. Leaving, he noticed a photograph on Soto's nightstand. A small photograph in a silver frame of an attractive middle-aged woman standing between two teenage boys, both of whom looked like Michael Soto, sleek and darkly handsome even at that raw age. He guessed it was Soto with his mother and twin brother, even though the woman happened to be blond and fair-skinned, clearly an Anglo. Did that mean Soto's father had been Hispanic?

Who was Soto? Now the question began to interest him.

But the clock on the nightstand reminded him of the time. Nearly seven. Estelle would be furious.

He wondered if he should call her. Or would calling now, at this late hour, upset her even more? Unable to decide, he retraced his steps to the desk in the living room. When he saw he red light on the phone, he thought for a moment that Estelle might be trying to reach him.

A crazy idea. How would she know where to find him?

He called the front desk.

"Let's see...yeah, Soto has a message from yesterday," the desk clerk said. "Call Reno."

"Reno?" he was confused. "The city of Reno?"

"I don't know. Call Reno. That's all it says."

He scribbled the message on a notepad by the phone and stuffed the piece of paper in his shirt pocket. Did Soto have a black market connection in Reno, Nevada? Another gallery owner, or a private dealer? Other possibilities came to mind. Gambling and drug smuggling and who knew what else.

Suddenly a stolen ahayu:da seemed like small change.

5

They were having tea at the kitchen table, as was their custom each night after dinner dishes had been washed and put away.

After scolding him for being late, Estelle had asked about his whereabouts and why he hadn't bothered to phone. As usual, she followed each question with silence measured out in solemn doses during dinner until he felt sufficiently guilty to apologize for his thoughtlessness.

"I'm sorry, Estelle, you're right, I should have called," he'd said to her finally. For the moment they seemed to be at peace, thanks to the ritual of reconciliation they'd developed over thirty-six years of marriage—having tea together at the kitchen table.

"Want some fruit?" She offered a plate of freshly sliced melon across the flowered tablecloth.

"No, I think I'll just have the tea tonight."

Estelle nodded, removing the stainless steel tea ball from her cup and placing it in a small ceramic bowl she kept on the table just for that purpose. She drank only chamomile tea, except she referred to it in Spanish as "manzanilla." She bought the tea in bulk from the herb shop down on Guadalupe Street, a small natural food store operated by a man who called himself Santa Fe's only "Herb Doctor." Estelle refused to buy commercial products like Celestial Seasonings. Only manzanilla from the Herb Doctor would satisfy her.

He sipped his Lipton, his tea of choice. Was he as rigid and set in his ways as Estelle? He supposed so, though he preferred to think otherwise. They might not have much to say to one another anymore, but they still enjoyed spending time together. Their marriage had changed over the years, as all marriages do. Though he enjoyed their quiet affection, he missed the passion they'd experienced in their youth. Sometimes it seemed to him that too much of their lives had become habit. Estelle probably felt the same way. But wasn't that to be expected, after all these years?

In truth, he would not change anything about their marriage which was as successful as any he knew. Over the years he had never once doubted that Estelle was as dedicated to him as he was to her.

He sighed when the telephone rang, interrupting their quiet time together. Estelle got up to answer as cheerfully as she did most everything. She brushed the wrinkles out of her skirt and straightened her cotton turtleneck, as though to make herself presentable. But to whom? He could tell by the tone of her voice that one of their daughters was calling, probably Flavia, since Adela usually called on weekends.

Estelle turned back to him. "It's Flavia," she said, as though to include him in the conversation. He watched her walk around the kitchen speaking and laughing into the cordless phone, jealous of her energy and animation.

Her energy never ceased to amaze him. No doubt about it, women aged better than men. Estelle was proof of that. She'd put on some weight, especially around the hips, and her once dark hair had turned a deep charcoal color that was even more noticeable now that she wore her hair long. But unlike him, her face showed little signs of wear. No furrows, no deep wrinkles under the eyes, no tired, sagging skin. Somehow she'd managed to preserve her youthfulness.

"We'd love to come," Estelle said, beginning to open and close the kitchen cabinets, the solid pine cabinets that her brother Larry had built and installed this past summer when they had modernized the kitchen. He tried to figure out why she kept opening and closing the cabinets. Was she looking for something? "How about Sunday after mass?" she asked, after a long pause.

He grimaced at the mention of mass. Estelle still acted as though her family attended mass every Sunday, when in fact he hadn't accompanied her in years. He also knew that Flavia and her husband went to services only on special occasions, Easter Sunday and Christmas Eve mostly.

He waited until she hung up the phone. "What's all that about?"

"Flavia and Luis want to show us their house. They finished decorating."

"We've already seen the house. Why do we need to see the decorations?"

Estelle ignored him, returning to the table and her lukewarm cup of tea. "Shall I heat some more water?"

He shook his head, thinking about the house Flavia and Luis had built in Tesuque on a hill overlooking the Santa Fe Opera. Rather extravagant for his taste, although Flavia and Luis could afford such extravagance, both of them being lawyers. Flavia worked for the Legislative Council, drafting bills for the members of the New Mexico legislature, and Luis happened to be a trial lawyer associated with one of the largest legal firms in Santa Fe.

He wasn't fond of Luis, as Estelle knew. He found him too slick, too concerned with status and social standing. The kind of person who went out of his way to let people know he'd reached such a level of prominence that he was "invited to all the right parties," as he liked to boast.

He much preferred his other son-in-law, Richard, but as fate would have it, Richard and Adela moved ninety miles away to Las Vegas, New Mexico. Flavia and Luis stayed in Santa Fe.

Were two daughters ever so different? He supposed the phenomenon was not uncommon. Still, he marveled at how different the two girls turned out. Flavia, the oldest, was more independent and self-centered, more aggressive.

Adela, three years younger, was more concerned with family, with making all the relationships work. Unlike Flavia, the fast track never interested Adela. After graduating in the same class from the University of New Mexico, both she and her husband took teaching jobs in the Las Vegas public schools. Adela taught second grade, while Richard taught biology in one of the junior highs and coached the school baseball team. They had two small children, Armando and Michele, who rode to school with Adela every morning and came back with her every afternoon.

He doubted that Flavia and Luis would ever slow down long enough to have kids. Maybe it would be better that way. He knew he hadn't been the greatest father in the world, having been absent so often because of his work. But Luis? He couldn't imagine Luis as a father.

Or Flavia as a mother, for that matter.

"You shouldn't be so hard on Luis," Estelle said. "He means well enough. He loves Flavia."

He nodded. He couldn't argue with that. Luis seemed to be a decent husband, the kind of husband Flavia needed, anyway.

He helped Estelle clear the table, and then out of habit he went outside for a cigarette, except now that he'd stopped smoking, sort of, he just sat on the porch bench and looked at their rose garden. His smoking had become such a sore spot between them that he dared not smoke anywhere in or around their house. Even in his study, with the door closed and the windows open, Estelle still complained about the smoke, which she claimed had fouled the air in their bedroom next door.

"I can't breathe," she would say as she climbed into bed, grabbing her throat and acting out her distress with such histrionics that he could not help but feel guilty. So he finally gave up smoking at the house altogether, not even an emergency cigarette. He wasn't sure if Estelle knew he kept a pack of Camel Lights handy, just in case, and he certainly wasn't planning to tell her.

From the veranda he saw a full moon rising over the Sangre de Cristo Mountains east of the city. Moonlight sparkled, reflecting off the leaves of the old cottonwood tree in the front yard. He smelled the dry leaves, just beginning to turn, and the scent of Piñon smoke drifting lazily from the chimneys of the houses along Acequia Madre Street. It was a pleasant night, even with the late August chill that marked the coming change of season. Soon nighttime temperatures would plunge below freezing and snow would start falling.

No doubt about it, winter cold and snow would be here soon enough. A sobering thought for someone who dreaded winter as much as he did. He sat on the wooden bench and leaned back against the thick adobe wall of the house, relaxing. It had been a long tiring day, and he had little to show for it other than a sore elbow, a headache, and a bunch of regrets for pushing Billy Suino. He certainly hadn't made any progress in finding out who—or what—killed Michael Soto.

A small car speeding down Acequia Madre interrupted his thoughts. It sounded like a BMW or one of the other speedy imports that people who lived on Santa Fe's fashionable East Side inevitably drove.

Living on the East Side had become something of an embarrassment for Fernando. He knew Estelle felt the same way, even if she pretended not to notice how the neighborhood had changed since 1970, the year they bought the house for a few thousand dollars. Yes, the neighborhood had changed since 1970. Their sleepy little enclave of mostly Spanish families no longer existed. That way of life seemed like a dream now, a fairy tale. It was as though they woke up one morning and found themselves living in an unreal community of rich and famous people from faraway places like New York and Los Angeles. Millionaires and movie stars.

Knowing his house had become something of an eyesore on Acequia Madre gave him a certain amount of pleasure. The other houses on the street had been sold and resold several times during the last forty years, what amounted to a frenzy of buying, renovating, and selling. And the frenzy continued. Already this year he and Estelle had received letters from a particular real estate agent claiming to have a client willing to pay, sight unseen, twice the appraised value for their small, modest adobe. The client turned out to be a Japanese businessman with a name like Yokomoto. Talk about historical irony. First the Spanish, then the Anglos, and now the Japanese. Fernando thought it was funny. Sort of.

What was the appraised value of their house? He had no idea. Predictably, Flavia and Luis advised them to take the money and run. "Why don't you buy a nice, cozy condo and retire?" Flavia asked, when they showed her one of the letters. "Because we don't want to live in a nice, cozy condo," he responded. Estelle gave him a dirty look and later told him he had been too harsh on the girl.

Maybe he had been too harsh. Flavia simply didn't

understand. She didn't have the same values. But why should she be expected to have the same values he and Estelle had? Fernando began to feel chilled. He'd forgotten to put on a jacket. His memory seemed to get worse every day. Estelle had said so just that morning. Maybe she was right.

Returning to the kitchen, he found Estelle talking on the telephone again. Someone from her church, he guessed, from the tone of her voice and the topic of conversation—a bake sale to be held sometime in October.

Estelle raised her hand, as if to indicate that she was too busy to be disturbed. He grunted, walking back to his study and ignoring the faded walls of the hallway, badly in need of a fresh coat of paint. Estelle wanted to have the work done immediately, but he had put it off for the time being. He wanted to wait until he retired so that he could do the work himself.

The windows of his study faced west, overlooking what used to be the Benavidez house and orchard. A young couple lived there now. Fernando rarely saw the husband, who worked day and night, six or seven days a week. He did see the wife, though.

Every morning she came outside at dawn wearing brightly colored tights or leotards. She always followed the same routine. First she pranced around her flowerbeds as though pretending to be a harem dancer. Finally she stood perfectly still for a few moments and then began to move in slow motion, one of those exercises that people did in Japan or Korea, places like that.

He closed the door behind him and opened the windows wide. Maybe Estelle wouldn't notice the cool air tonight, being preoccupied with her phone calls. Then he sat down and turned on his desk lamp. The room looked much the same as when Flavia and Adela had used it as a bedroom. He'd given away the twin beds, but he hadn't bothered to change the pink wallpaper or take down the watercolor paintings left over from Adela's art classes at Santa Fe High.

Sitting at the desk relaxed him. He loved this room. He remembered tiptoeing in to kiss the girls goodnight, long after they'd fallen asleep. Maybe that was why he hadn't changed the wallpaper or tossed Adela's watercolors—because all those little things reminded him of the good years when the girls were growing up and he and Estelle were young together. Hard years, financially. But he no longer complained about the hardship, no longer kidded himself. He would take those early years back in a second, if only he could.

Feelings of loss mingled with simple exhaustion. He should not allow himself to get so tired. He knew better.

The day had left him with an unsettled feeling. Soto's murder troubled him, not because he didn't have enough information to solve the crime. That would come, in due time.

What bothered him was something else—the fear, however vague, that solving the mystery of Soto's death would take him down a road he did not want to travel, take him to the dark underside of history, all the irrational fears and violent impulses that led to racial hatred and cultural warfare.

He'd always been one to take the easy way out, the path of least resistance. Now Soto's murder threatened to make that option impossible, threatened to bring all the hatred to the surface. How else could he explain his angry confrontations with Suiño and Padilla? He couldn't remember the last time he'd lost his temper and actually tried to hurt someone. Not prone to excessive behavior of any kind, he'd never had a weakness for violence.

So why, then, did Suiño and Padilla both disturb him so deeply? Just because he worked within the system didn't mean he'd turned against the People, but maybe he'd made a mistake by overlooking the hatred that existed below the placid surface of Santa Fe. Maybe he'd repressed too much. Feeling even more agitated, he opened the bottom drawer of the desk and thumbed through the manila folders until he found what he wanted. He placed the thin folder under the desk lamp and flipped through the photocopied pages he'd obtained last year from the New Mexico State Records Center and Archives.

He examined the pages carefully, as though looking for something he'd missed earlier. The pages represented a detailed inventory of the 1630 Mission Supply Train that his relative, Salvador de Lopez, accompanied from Mexico City to Santa Fe along the route known as the Camino Real. Salvador was mentioned only once, and only insofar as he and the other nine soldiers accompanying the Supply Train had been paid 270 pesos in common gold.

They came on wagons overburdened with barrels and crates, wagons that had to be pulled by alternating teams of mules, eight pulling and eight resting. Many settlers died along the way, and those who survived led lives of unspeakable hardship. Unlike the English, who as they colonized along the East Coast exterminated entire Indian tribes because they believed the souls of "savages" belonged to the devil, the Spanish actively cultivated the souls of the Indians they encountered, trying to enlist them in the cause of Christianity.

Sure, events had turned out poorly, as they so often did. The march of civilization had quickly become an orgy of butchery and exploitation. He would not deny that. But the original intent had not been to destroy. He insisted on remembering that—the nobility of the intent, alongside the evil of what had actually transpired.

Out of the corner of his eye he noticed a shadow in the hallway. It was Estelle, standing in the darkness. How long had she been watching him? What did she want?

"Are you coming to bed, Fernando?" she asked, waiting for his response.

He tried to see the expression on Estelle's face, but the hallway was too dark.

"Coming," he said, closing the manila folder. Then he turned off the desk lamp and went to join his wife.

6

He couldn't believe his bad luck. Not even the glare of the morning sunshine slanting down on San Ildefonso Pueblo could disguise the unwanted sight of Trujillo. Leaning against the hood of his black Santa Fe County Sheriff's car, Trujillo raised his hand as he approached on the narrow blacktop and then drove into the south plaza. It was not a greeting so much as a command to stop.

Trujillo's presumptuousness reminded him of all the things he didn't like about this football player turned deputy sheriff.

It was especially galling this morning, because he'd come out to San Ildefonso a full forty-five minutes earlier than the prearranged time so that he could talk to Sammy Tso and Dora Alvarez by himself, without the macho presence of Trujillo.

Trujillo's jaw dropped when he realized he wasn't going to stop. The confused, slightly hurt look on the younger man's face partially compensated him for his irritation. He drove to the end of the dusty plaza and parked in front of the tribal office, next to a new model Chevy Blazer with so many dents and broken windows that it looked like someone had tried to remodel it with a sledge-hammer.

When he heard Trujillo's footsteps, he stood up and stretched his stiff back. Today he'd remembered his sunglasses, so he didn't feel so bad looking into Trujillo's Ray-Bans.

The younger man seemed out of breath, maybe pissed. He couldn't tell which.

"I thought you said ten o'clock?"

He frowned. "That's right, ten o'clock. You're early."

He walked into the tribal office and removed his sunglasses, letting his eyes adjust to the semi-dark interior. Down a long windowless hallway was a photocopying machine and, at the very end, the door to the governor's office. The woman sitting behind the information counter looked up from her newspaper and motioned toward the sign hanging on the wall beside a map of the pueblo. The sign listed the entrance fees tourists were required to pay before entering the pueblo, as well as camera and artist fees for those wishing to photograph or sketch on pueblo land.

He ignored the sign. "I'm Detective Fernando Lopez from the Santa Fe Police Department. We're looking for Sammy Tso and Dora Alvarez. I believe they live in the pueblo."

The woman peered over the top of her reading glasses, first at him and then at Trujillo, who stood back near the door.

She had a round face and short dark hair that looked as though it had been permed into tight curls.

After a considerable silence, she asked, "What's the problem?"

"No problem. I'd like to ask them some questions. Just routine stuff."

"You have no jurisdiction here. If this is a matter for the Tribal Police, then—"

"No, please, that won't be necessary. Really, I only want to ask for their help. They might have information about a man who lives in Jacoñita. Someone we're looking for."

Though technically false, this last statement wasn't impossibly far from the truth, he told himself. Whatever happened, he wanted to avoid having to work with the Tribal Police. Who had the patience for collaborating with the damned Tribal Police? Not him, and certainly not Trujillo.

The woman continued to stare at them, considering what to do. He held his breath, hoping Trujillo wouldn't open his mouth and blurt out something hostile that would ruin whatever chance they had with this woman.

"And you say Sammy and Dora are not suspects?"

"No, I only want to ask for their help, nothing more than that."

When he saw the woman begin to nod her head, he suspected they were home free. If Trujillo could keep his mouth shut.

"Dora lives on the north side of the pueblo by the cottonwood tree." She pointed in the general direction of Black Mesa. "Sammy's harder to find. He lives in a trailer down by the river. You go back out the highway and take a right on the last dirt road before the gate. Follow it down to the river. His is the last trailer before the river."

"I appreciate your help."

Even Trujillo muttered a begrudging "thank you" before opening the door and stepping outside.

He followed, fumbling with his sunglasses as he walked into sunshine so intense it transformed the scene before him into a faded watercolor—tan adobe, turquoise doors and window frames, pink earth packed as hard as rock.

Once again he imagined his eyes fogging up with cataracts. Could he really sense his eyesight getting weaker? After listening to Estelle's horror stories, who wouldn't be paranoid?

Trujillo shook his head and motioned back toward the tribal office.

"Like pulling teeth."

They walked across the plaza, past the round wall of the great kiva with its adobe steps leading up to an opening in the roof where a ladder made from stripped tree branches provided entrance to the underground chamber below. The tips of the poles extended a good twenty feet above the kiva, reaching into the blue sky.

He steered clear of the kiva, well aware that outsiders were strictly forbidden access to these secret chambers. Exactly what religious ceremonies took place in the kivas remained a mystery to him and all the other Spanish and Anglo latecomers.

In fact, they knew precious little about pueblo religion, even after 450 long years of cohabitation, sometimes peaceful and sometimes not.

He had to give the pueblos credit. They knew how to keep a secret.

When they entered the older part of San Ildefonso, built around the north plaza, a shaggy black and white border collie trotted up to greet them. The dog wagged its tail and whimpered.

"Get away, mutt!" Trujillo snapped at the dog. The collie stopped, bared its teeth, and backed away.

He shrugged and then pointed to the tall cottonwood tree that towered over the one-story adobe buildings clustered around the plaza. The doors and windows of the buildings were painted bright blue to keep away evil spirits. That was the tradition. Two or three hundred yards beyond the cottonwood loomed the massive, omnipresent shape of Black Mesa. It was a slab of black rock, like the navel of a gigantic beast that lay just below the earth's surface, waiting to spring to life.

To the left of the cottonwood tree was a small, rectangular adobe, its outer layer of stucco faded to the color of dust. Huge cracks in the stucco revealed the mud and straw bricks underneath, partially disintegrated from long exposure to the elements. Goats wandered freely around the unfenced yard, grazing on patches of cheat grass and weeds. They ignored their approach, but not the old woman sitting on an old car seat under the cottonwood tree. Her eyes followed them every step of the way.

He cringed at the sight of the old woman's face, wrinkled beyond recognition from too many years in the sun. Did his face look this winkled to other people, as Estelle claimed? The thought depressed him as he walked into the welcome shade of the cottonwood and nodded politely to the old woman.

Before he could speak, he noticed a seat belt fastened around the woman's waist, fitting snugly over her black dress.

The seat belt confused him. Why would someone bring an old woman out here and put her in a seat belt? So she wouldn't wander off by herself? "Dora Alvarez?"

The old woman stared at him with unblinking eyes. Her mouth puckered in layers of wrinkles.

He tried again. "I'm looking for Dora Alvarez."

Finally the woman muttered something in Tewa, the dialect of the Tanoan language spoken at San Ildefonso. He had learned to distinguish Tewa from the other two Tanoan dialects, and from the Keresan language spoken by the southern pueblos and the Zuni language spoken by the Zunis. But distinguishing one dialect from another didn't mean he could understand any of them.

"Excuse me?"

The old woman slowly raised her arm and pointed to the house, her hand shaking uncontrollably.

"*Gracias,*" he said, thinking she might understand Spanish better than English.

The sight of Trujillo already banging on the screen door annoyed him. Dealing with these people required some delicacy. Trujillo just didn't get it.

"Wait, let me ask the questions." He joined Trujillo on the slab concrete porch. "I have a lot of experience out here."

Trujillo didn't respond, but he stepped back, making room for him. Somewhat surprised, he wondered if Trujillo had begun to feel out of his element. He hated to give the younger man that much credit.

A plump woman who looked to be in her late forties appeared on the other side of the screen door. She wiped her hands on a cotton apron tied around her dress. "Yes?"

"Dora Alvarez?"

The woman nodded, looking at them suspiciously with the biggest, blackest eyes he had ever seen. Bedroom eyes.

He introduced himself. "I wonder if you could help me with some information about the peyote meeting in Jacoñita this past weekend." He gave the woman a big smile, the biggest he could muster. "I hate to bother you like this, but if you could just tell me what you saw that night, it would be a big help."

Her eyes narrowed at the mention of the peyote ceremony. She didn't bother to hide her unease.

"It'll only take a few minutes of your time."

The woman sighed and opened the screen door.

"Thank you, you don't know how much I appreciate this."

He followed her inside, taking stock of the one-room house as quickly as he could without being too conspicuous.

He noticed two double beds along the far wall and a sitting area in the center of the room facing a small kiva fireplace.

Directly ahead a small boy sat at the kitchen table eating a buttered flour tortilla. The child continued to eat, round face and big brown eyes, staring over the top of his tortilla at the two strangers standing awkwardly in his house. Yellow globs of melted butter dripped down from the tortilla onto the boy's oversized Hard Rock Cafe T-shirt.

"Let me finish what I'm doing."

She returned to the wood-burning stove where she'd been making tortillas. She rolled out the last of her dough, placed it in a tortilla press, and then tossed the tortilla on a cast-iron grill. She flipped it once, quickly, and then wrapped it in a towel with the others.

He smelled the steam rising from the warm tortillas and suddenly felt hungry, a burning sensation in the pit of his stomach. He should have eaten something this morning. Coffee just wasn't enough to get him through the day.

Why hadn't he stopped at Burger King on his way out to San Ildefonso? Too late now.

"Have a seat." She untied her apron and hung it on a handle attached to the front of the stove.

He sat downt at the kitchen table, directly across from the boy, while Trujillo, keeping his distance, sat in one of the wooden chairs near the fireplace. He noticed the kitchen cabinets, freshly painted with a thick coat of red enamel. Counter tops, too. The red paint brightened what to him seemed like an otherwise gloomy room. The heavy black stove and the cast-iron pots hanging from the ceiling beams didn't help the ambiance any.

After straightening the front of her dress, the woman sat down next to him. She placed her hands in her lap and waited, her dark round face expressionless, impassive.

He felt uncomfortable. "Okay, I appreciate you taking the time to answer a few questions. As you know, Michael Soto was murdered during the ceremony night before last. I wonder if you could tell me what you saw that night, when the peyote meeting broke up and this...this intruder appeared." He saw the wrinkles around the woman's eyes suddenly tighten. She continued to stare at him.

"Did you get a good look at the man who disrupted the ceremony?"

"Not a man," she said. "A wolfman. Maybe a skinwalker, like the Navajo say. Mai tso. Yenaldlooshi."

He recognized the common Navajo name for skinwalker, a

dreaded mythic beast, half man and half wolf. Local superstition maintained that skinwalkers could run and fly supernaturally fast, changing shapes at will, from human to animal form. Skinwalkers caused sickness and death, as well as despair and a host of other evils.

"A wolfman or a skinwalker?" He wanted to be sure he heard the woman correctly. He hoped he hadn't. He had enough trouble already.

She nodded.

"What did he look like?"

"Like he always looks. Big man with the head of a wolf. Bent over."

"Then you've seen him before?"

Again she nodded. "Sometimes at night we hear him out on the mesa. He comes at night to eat the goats. When you run out to shoot him, he changes into a crow and flies away. In the morning you find the goats he's eaten. He doesn't offer a prayer or a sacrifice. He eats them alive and carries them around so their blood drips on the ground, and where the blood drips nothing ever grows from the earth, not even sage or rabbit bush."

"You think it's the same wolfman?"

She shrugged, a blank expression on her face.

Over in the rocking chair Trujillo rolled his eyes.

He ignored Trujillo. "His face. What exactly does it look like?"

"Like a wolf. Big white fangs and a red tongue. Sometimes he has blood dripping from his teeth. Lots of blood."

He closed his eyes and rubbed his forehead. He was getting bad vibes again.

"And sometimes you hear a sound in the night, and you look out and see his eyes glowing in the dark."

"Have any of these wolfmen ever tried to harm you?"

She nodded, sadly. "Once we heard one on the roof. That's when my husband got sick and died a week later. Two years ago."

"This wolfman at the peyote meeting, he walked into the teepee, right?"

"I guess so."

"And he ran out after Michael Soto, correct?"

"No, he changed into a crow and flew out the door," she said.

"What?" He scratched his head. "Are you sure he changed shape?"

"I remember the sound of his wings beating against the canvas, and his voice, the voice of the crow. Croaking."

He rubbed his tired eyes. "Croaking?"

The woman nodded.

Trying to get the image of a wolfman changing into a crow out of his mind, he asked, "What happened next? After Soto and the crow ran or flew out of the teepee?"

"We were scared, so we stayed in the teepee. When we heard the shot, a couple of minutes later, Road Chief went to see what happened and came back to tell us. I got so upset when I heard the wolfman killed Michael Soto, you know, I had to leave. So Sammy Tso took me home then. Back here. Maybe twelve thirty, quarter to one."

"Do you know the name of Road Chief and the other officers?"

"José Padilla," she said. "He was Fire Chief."

"Yes, I know, but what about the others?"

She shook her head. "I don't know their names, but I saw them drive up to José's house in their van. Big gray van with the teepee poles on top. Four men, all together in the van."

He paused. "Four men? I'm not sure I understand. Did you see five people in the van—four men in addition to Peyote Woman, Road Chief's wife? I know about Road Chief, Cedar Chief, and Drummer Chief, but who was the fourth man?"

She stared at him, a look of confusion on her face. "Maybe not. I forgot about Peyote Woman. Must have been only three men and one woman in the van."

He sighed, taking a small notebook out of his shirt pocket and writing down his name and phone number. "If you see this wolfman again, give me a call. Maybe I can help."

She looked horrified at the suggestion.

Standing, he saw Trujillo already at the door waiting for him. They thanked her and then went outside where the old woman still sat buckled to her car seat under the cottonwood.

He adjusted his sunglasses and marched quickly across the

plaza, ignoring the laughter of Trujillo, who followed a few steps behind.

Trujillo might find this wolfman business funny, but not him. Superstitions ceased to be funny when they mucked up an already complicated investigation. Especially a superstition as prevalent as this, one accepted as fact by most people around here. And anyway, who could say with absolute certainty that wolfmen and skinwalkers did not exist? How a person defined fact depended on cultural perspective, as he had learned over the years. The hard way.

"Watch out for werewolves," Trujillo quipped, coming up beside him.

"I wonder. What if we don't see these things because we don't believe in them and so don't know what to look for?"

Trujillo laughed. "You've had too much sun."

"Probably."

By the time they reached the parking lot near the tribal office he felt slightly dizzy. He desperately needed some food, or at least another cup of coffee, but that would have to wait until the return trip to Santa Fe.

First they had to find Sammy Tso and listen to his version of what had happened Sunday night at Jacoñita. He would likely tell more tall tales of mythic beasts, or maybe something entirely different, since so far the investigation had produced more contradictions than common ground.

"I'll follow you," Trujillo said, heading for his car.

He climbed into his green unmarked Plymouth and revved the big engine. He drove out to the paved road, where he waited for Trujillo to catch up, and then followed the two-lane blacktop that curved gracefully through red hills dotted with piñon and junper trees. Less than a hundred yards from the main entrance to San Ildefonso a dirt road cut off sharply to the right. He slammed on his brakes, screeched to a stop, and proceeded cautiously along the bumpy road, made treacherous by a network of deep ruts. The road hadn't been graded and graveled after the July rainy season, as normal maintenance would require.

Whoever lived down here didn't expect—or want—many visitors.

Along the way they passed the ruins of a tiny adobe whose roof had collapsed. Parked out back, a classic 1951 International pickup had long since rusted to a dull brown color.

Finally, over a small rise, the road sloped down toward the Rio Grande, its banks clearly delineated by a thick growth of tamarisk, willow, and salt bush.

Tso's mobile home stood among a scattering of outbuildings and corrals, with a strip of well-tended fields extending north along the lush riverbank. The obvious prosperity surprised him.

When he parked near the first corral, two dark brown horses wandered over to the barbed wire fence expecting to be fed. Their ears perked up hopefully, pathetically. He let the horses prance around for a few short seconds, snorting and whinnying, then slammed the car door to scare the animals away. He'd never liked horses, not even as a kid. Big, dangerous, stupid animals too nervous and high strung to be tolerated by anyone with any sense.

Predictably, Trujillo went directly to the fence and began to rub one of the horses behind its ears. "Good looking quarter horses."

He headed for the river, toward where a lone figure worked in one of the adjoining fields. As he walked along the irrigation ditch, he noticed a woman and two small children staring at him from the doorway of the mobile home. Tso's wife and kids? They didn't look particularly happy to see a couple of Hispanic cops trespassing on their property.

Neither did the man standing in the field. He waited impassively, holding a five-gallon plastic bucket filled with yellow squash. The man looked about his age, wearing a red headband that kept the long black bangs out of his eyes.

Tso's father? Or father-in-law?

"Morning. Sorry to bother you. I'm looking for Sammy Tso. He might be able to help me out with some information."

"Trouble with the law?" the man asked, squinting into the sun, his face the color of saddle leather.

"No trouble. I'm here to ask for his help."

The man shook his head, not convinced. "Sammy's not here. He hasn't been home since Sunday. We've been looking for him, too."

He noticed the man glance back toward the road. Then he saw why. A red Toyota pickup was approaching, bouncing over the dirt road, leaving a huge cloud of dust behind it. Did the light on the Toyota's roof indicate Tribal Police? He couldn't decide. Maybe the woman back at the tribal office had changed her mind and given them a call.

"Shit!" He turned away from the man with the red headband and hurried back along the irrigation ditch. He made it back to his car just as the Toyota pulled into the yard.

Trujillo stood alongside his black cruiser, scowling at the two men in the Toyota.

The driver spoke. "What do you want? You have no jurisdiction here."

"Nothing, we're just leaving," he said quickly, hoping Trujillo could shut up long enough for the two of them to extricate themselves from a potentially sticky situation.

The driver, wearing a black cowboy hat and reflecting sunglasses, stepped out of the Toyota and removed his sunglasses. His partner cradled a shotgun in his lap.

He shouted at Trujillo. "Let's go!"

Trujillo remained defiant, standing with his hands firmly planted on his hips. His right hand rested on his black leather holster.

Great, he thought, a shoot-out at San Ildefonso. That's just what we need, a fucking shoot-out.

"Trujillo! Get in the car."

Acting fast, he turned and took a step toward the Plymouth. He was about to take a second when a blow on the back of his head sent him reeling to the ground. He tasted dirt and something else, blood, in his mouth.

"Hey!"

Trujillo rushed at the driver but stopped dead in his tracks when he saw the man's partner pointing his shotgun at them. He was older than the driver, wearing a leather vest over his bare chest, with a long braid of black hair hanging down his back.

"Get the fuck out of here, both of you," the driver said. He meant business, a mean motherfucker.

He fumbled in the dirt trying to get his bearings. Regaining his senses slowly, he turned over and sat up. Trujillo helped him to his feet. "Yeah, don't mind if I do."

The two Indians watched them climb into their cars. Trujillo squealed off in his cruiser, while he fought to find his keys. When he did, he hit the ignition, backed up, and swerved into a shallow ditch and then back onto the dirt road.

Mercifully, the Indians didn't follow. He caught a last glimpse of them standing beside the Toyota pickup watching from behind their mirrored sunglasses.

7

He walked into the Washington Avenue station with a massive headache and a scowl on his face. What did he have to show for his efforts at San Ildefonso? Tall tales of skinwalkers and wolfmen told by a cast of witnesses who would cause District Attorney Steve Chabot to throw up his hands in despair and tell Fernando to get the hell out of his office and don't come back until you have something I can fucking use! He had heard it all before. He didn't need to hear it again.

So far today the only productive thing he'd done was to ditch Trujillo at the Burger King in Nambé, where they'd stopped for a greasy lunch and a couple of Tylenol for his headache. He'd managed to dust himself off and clean most of the dirt off his face in the Burger King restroom, but not to erase the memory of the tough guy who sucker punched him back at San Ildefonso. Whoever the guy was, he couldn't have been tribal police. No tribal officer would do that to a fellow cop.

"Jesus, Fernando, you look like shit," Linda said from behind the front counter. "But hey, cheer up, you're a popular man today."

"Yeah?" he grunted, glancing routinely at the police blotter. "So what do you have for me?"

"Preliminary lab report," she said, handing him a computer printout. "And someone called. Oh hell, I wrote it down somewhere." She searched through a stack of telephone slips in the wire basket on the counter. "Here it is—Sammy Tso wants you to call him. He'll be at this number until one o'clock."

The name took him by surprise. "Sammy Tso? I was just looking for him out at San Ildefonso."

"He sounded urgent, if you know what I mean. Like he really wanted to talk." Linda handed him the slip of paper.

He took the lab report and the telephone message down the ugly brown hall to his office, wondering why Tso had changed his mind and decided to come out of hiding. Maybe he wanted to confess to Soto's murder.

Yeah, that would be the day.

But Tso would have to wait, he decided. After all, his disappearing act had almost precipitated a shootout between Tomas Trujillo and the San Ildefonso Tribal Police or whoever they were. Let the *pendejo* wait a few more minutes. It would serve him right.

He scanned the preliminary lab report, quickly realizing the utter uselessness of the report.

Unfortunately, the results of the ballistic tests were not yet available. So far the wizards at the lab had been able to establish the presence of wool and denim microfibers on the rear seat of Soto's Porsche and to find about two dozen sets of footprints in Padilla's driveway. None of the fingerprints in the car matched any known scumbags. Wool and denim microfibers and two dozen sets of footprints would really narrow their list of suspects. If, that is, they had any suspects.

He tossed the printout on the stack of papers at the rear of his desk and called Tso.

"El Nido," a man answered the phone on the first ring.

He hesitated. He remembered a restaurant in Tesuque called El Nido. Other than that he drew a blank. "Hello—I'm calling Sammy Tso. He gave me this number."

"Okay, just a minute."

Someone picked up the phone. "Lopez?" The voice sounded youthful.

"Speaking."

"I heard you were looking for me this morning."

Tso paused, waiting for a reply. When none was forthcoming, he continued. "Well...I'm ready to talk...I wanted you to know."

Why so nervous? he wondered, listening to the kid stammer. Tso sounded like a kid, at any rate. He was much too young to be involved in peyote ceremonies and murder.

"Do you still want to talk?"

"Yeah, as a matter of fact I do."

"Can you come out here? I'll wait for you in the bar."

He didn't relish the idea of driving out to Tesuque, but what else could he do with Tso all gift-wrapped and waiting for him at El Nido? He couldn't refuse this bit of good luck, especially since his luck had been running the other way for longer than he cared to remember.

"I'll be there in fifteen minutes."

"Okay. Uh...Lopez...you don't think I killed Soto, do you?"

The bluntness of the question amused him. What did the kid expect him to say? "Why, do you want to confess?" he asked, unable to completely hide his sarcasm.

"No. I had nothing to do with it...that's why I called...to explain."

"I'll be there in fifteen minutes."

Before leaving, he went to the closet in the back of his office and changed shirts. He stuffed his soiled shirt in a gym bag he kept in the closet and replaced it with another of the white, polyester blend, non-wrinkle shirts Estelle bought for him. When he was younger, he occasionally wore a necktie. Now he didn't give a damn how he looked.

"Leaving so soon?" Linda asked as he walked up to the front counter.

"I'm going out to El Nido to meet Sammy Tso."

He crossed the street to the parking lot and climbed into his Plymouth. With one hand on the steering wheel, he drove out of the lot and turned right on Washington Avenue. Beyond the Paseo, Washington became Bishop's Lodge Road, which took him past Fort Marcy Park and Bishop's Lodge, then down into Tesuque Canyon, with the new age solar adobes of the rich Anglos who lived there packed tightly between the red clay hills on either side of the highway. Just beyond the Shidoni Foundry he came to El Nido, a sprawling adobe building with a portal in front and two wings jutting off to either side of the main entrance.

He turned into the gravel parking lot and walked up the front steps. Inside the restaurant area was blocked off, a chalkboard announcing that the restaurant would reopen at five p.m. and that tonight's specials would be "Blue Corn Chicken Enchilladas with Sour Cream" and "Trout å la Pinon Nuts." Thinking about the trout made him hungry. Maybe he would come back tonight with Estelle—they hadn't gone out to dinner for a couple of weeks. They needed to get out more often.

Walking into the bar, he spotted Tso immediately—a skinny Indian wearing skin-tight jeans, flashy concho belt, and a neon blue shirt made of silk or rayon, one of those slinky fabrics. Sipping a can of Pepsi, he sat alone at a table near the back window. The kid couldn't be more than twemty years old.

"Howdy," the bartender said, with a friendly smile plastered on his face, just above his charcoal gray goatee.

"Afternoon."

The bartender poured a tall shot of tequila for an old man sitting at the bar with his cowboy hat and pack of Lucky Strikes placed in front of him on the mahogany counter.

"Be right with you," the bartender said, as he walked back to meet Sammy Tso.

The kid nodded his head nervously, not offering to shake hands. He wore his hair in a long braid that reached the middle of his back.

He eased himself into one of the Mexican leather chairs at the table. "Sammy Tso, I assume." He noticed the kid's complexion was as smooth as a baby's.

"Why were you looking for me...if you don't think I killed Soto?"

"Whoa, slow down. I wanted to ask you a few questions, that's all."

The kid shrugged. "Okay...shoot."

He sighed. "You might start by telling me what you were doing at the peyote ceremony."

"I'm a member of the church."

He glanced again at the kid's designer western clothes. "You don't look like a member of the Native American Church."

"What's that supposed to mean?"

"Forget it." He frowned. "Tell me what you know about Michael Soto. Did he organize the meeting?"

Tso shook his head. "No way. Not Soto. He was new to the

area—he wasn't even a member of the church."

"So who did?"

"José Padilla and John Reno. They run the meetings together, the two of them."

For the first time that day he smiled. Padilla had been a lousy liar, in spite of his pretended indignation.

"So this John Reno guy was Road Chief?" He remembered the name from La Fonda, where Soto had a message to 'Call Reno.'

The kid nodded. "He lives near Gallup. I don't know him very well—I've only been a member of the church for a few months. He's a good friend of José's."

"Who were the other officials?"

"They came with Reno. Friends of his...or people who work for him, I don't know."

He frowned, having heard too many people plead ignorance of late. "So how many people did Reno bring with him?"

Tso's eyes narrowed. "Four. The other officials."

"Four men?"

"Yeah—I think so," Tso said, without much confidence. "No, wait, only three. Because one had to be Reno's wife, Peyote Woman."

While he considered, Tso sucked innocently on his straw.

Finally the bartender sauntered over to their table, a damp towel hung over his shoulder. "What can I get you?" he asked.

He checked his watch. "Give me a Modelo."

"Will do, partner." The bartender sauntered back to the bar as slowly as he had come.

As soon as the bartender returned, he poured the beer and watched it foam to the top of his mug. He drank the glass halfway down and sighed, enjoying the taste of the beer.

"Okay. What happened when the peyote meeting broke up? What did you see?"

Tso hesitated. "I didn't get a good look at him, the person who disrupted the meeting...if that's what you mean. Actually, I didn't see him at all. You have to understand...I'd eaten a lot of peyote, more than I usually do. Have you ever taken peyote?"

When he didn't respond, Tso continued. "You see things...

bright colors and visions...and sometimes it's hard to tell what's real from what's not."

He remained skeptical but said nothing.

"When we broke for the Midnight Water Call, I couldn't feel my legs. I remember staring into the fire and the colors shooting out at me like exploding stars...right at my face. I saw my grandmother...a vision of my grandmother, who died of T.B. when I was a kid. She told me about her journey...and that if I wanted to join her, I would have to follow my road. But then she started to cough and couldn't stop...her face turned black and shriveled to ashes.

"That's about when I heard the shouting outside the teepee—or maybe inside, I couldn't tell where it came from. The next thing I remember, José Padilla fell across my legs. See, because I was sitting next to him...so when he stumbled through the door, he fell on top of me. After that I don't know how long I lay there on my back. I heard the shouting, but I didn't really know what happened until later, when John Reno told us Michael Soto was dead."

"So Reno discovered the body?"

"Yeah, I guess," the kid said.

He shook his head, out of patience. "So what do you think—was the intruder a wolfman?"

Tso looked away.

"Or was he just a man wearing a wolf mask?"

The kid shrugged, still avoiding his eyes.

"You recognized him, didn't you?"

"No." The kid glanced at him for a brief second and then shifted uneasily in his chair.

He took a sip of beer and continued staring at the kid. "So tell me, why were you so eager to reach me this afternoon?"

"I didn't want you to think I killed Soto."

"Why would I think you killed Soto?"

Tso shrugged.

"Who did kill him?"

"I told you, I don't know," the kid pleaded.

"What was your relationship with Soto?" He could tell the question made the kid uncomfortable as soon as he asked it.

"What do you mean?"

"I mean why are you so nervous?" he said, raising his voice. He felt like shouting.

Tso started to get up and then changed his mind. "My relationship with Soto was only business."

"What kind of business? Selling tribal objects on the black market? Like Padilla?"

At that Tso did stand up, knocking his chair backwards. When it crashed to the floor, the bartender yelled across the room. "Take it easy, boys!"

The bartender and the old man at the bar stared at them, waiting to see what would happen next.

He reached over and pulled the chair upright. "That's what you do, isn't it? Sell what you can steal from your family and your tribe? Isn't that right, you little prick?"

"I don't have to listen to this." The kid headed for the door. "You got what you came for."

"Don't go far, I'll be in touch."

He grinned at the bartender and the old man. "These kids today—they don't have any respect."

Laughing, the bartender agreed. "You got that right."

He counted out five one dollar bills and left them on the table for the bartender, who nodded his appreciation. He stepped outside just in time to see Tso driving away, squealing out of the gravel parking lot in a white Toyota 4 x 4 pickup with a chrome roll-bar and oversize tires. The truck looked brand new, as if Tso had driven it off the showroom floor that very morning. No doubt about it, the kid had more than a little disposable income. Where he got the cash didn't strike him as any great mystery.

Watching the cloud of dust settle in the parking lot, he considered what to do next. His first impulse was to pay Padilla another friendly visit, but he decided against the short drive to Jacoñita. Before doing anything else he needed more information about John Reno. Padilla could wait.

He took his time driving into Santa Fe, ignoring the traffic that piled up behind him as he climbed out of Tesuque Canyon, the teenagers blaring their horns and shouting at him from the windows of their BMWs and Audi's. Let them shout, for all the good it would do. He had no patience for the precious, privileged kids of the wealthy Anglos who, even on the highway, expected to have everything their way.

Imagine growing up without limits—not having to recognize the rigid boundaries of class and race that separated people. Growing up with a sense of entitlement, the arrogance of feeling entitled to everything their parents' money could buy.

He had forgotten all about the teenagers by the time he pulled into the parking lot on Washington Avenue and walked into the station. Linda nodded, chatting on the phone in an unusually friendly tone of voice.

Linda winked at him and kept talking.

Once in his office he wasted no time. He buzzed Antonio and asked him to call Luisita Benavides, a friend of Antonio's who worked at the New Mexico Department of Motor Vehicles. He wanted an address for John Reno, and he wanted it fast. Benavides had always come through in the past, whenever they'd had reason to call.

"No problem," Antonio said.

Then, unfortunately, the waiting began. He hated waiting. He lacked the proper patience, or perhaps the temperament, whatever it was that allowed people to pass the time gracefully.

When Antonio walked into the office, he immediately sensed his black mood. "Cheer up, man. I have the information you wanted."

"Good man," he said, glad to get back to work so that he could keep his mind occupied.

Antonio handed him a slip of paper, then grabbed a metal chair, spun it around, and straddled it as though mounting a horse. "Benavides found two possibilities—a J. Reno in Truchas, and a John Reno in Whitewater."

Fernando smiled, looking at the addresses.

"I never liked Truchas. Too many hippies up there."

"No, I don't think we're interested in the Reno from Truchas," he said absently, searching through the clutter on his desk. Then, remembering, he opened the top drawer and brought out the "Guide to Indian Country" map he'd found in the glove compartment of Soto's Porsche.

He took his time unfolding the oversized map and moments later found himself looking once again at the circle, drawn with black marker, around the town of Whitewater, a few miles north of Zuni.

"Here." He shoved the map toward Antonio, who stared back at him, confused.

Before he could explain, the telephone buzzed. It turned out to be Linda, bearing the bad news that Tomas Trujillo was waiting for him on line five. What did Trujillo want now?

"Lopez here." He didn't bother to hide his irritation that Trujillo had called at such an inconvenient time.

"Didn't I tell you not to release him?"

"What are you talking about?"

"José Padilla, what do you think?"

Trujillo was clearly angry about something.

"I told you not to release him. Don't tell me you haven't heard. About an hour ago he was arrested trying to sell the ahayu:da to an art gallery in Taos."

He paused, taken completely by surprise. "Taos?"

"That's right, Taos. I'm bringing him and the ahayu:da back to Santa Fe this evening. Will you be there?"

"Yeah, okay."

"And Lopez, this time don't release him."

8

By tomorrow Padilla's swollen left eye would turn an ugly black and blue color. He hadn't asked for an explanation, preferring not to know the unpleasant details of Trujillo's tactics. Padilla sat meekly at the metal table, dwarfed by Trujillo on one side and Antonio on the other, both men staring at Padilla with their arms folded across their chests, forearms bulging. The intimidation seemed to be working, because the look of hostility on Padilla's face when he'd first arrived at the station had changed to something else.

Resignation, perhaps. Squeezed between the two huge cops, Padilla appeared much older and frailer than his fifty years.

He noticed the gray stubble growing on the little man's chin and the deep wrinkles in his forehead. He also noted that for his trip to Taos Padilla had exchanged his painter's uniform for chinos and a black polo shirt, more suitable for a business transaction.

A black shirt for selling a stolen ahayu:da on the black market. He liked the imagery.

Sitting at the far end of the long metal table opposite Padilla, he examined the ahayu:da Padilla had tried to sell. The woodcarving matched the Big Brother ahayu:da pictured in the Edward S. Curtis photograph that Fidel had shown him in the newsroom of the *Independent*. The same shrouded face, the same erect umbilical cord jutting out from its abdomen.

Except this one looked newer and less decomposed, the blond wood just beginning to turn gray. But what did he know, never having seen an actual ahayu:da before? He stopped playing with the woodcarving and turned to Padilla.

"So tell me, did Soto give you the ahayu:da to sell? Or did you take it when you killed him?"

"No!" Padilla shot back.

"So you killed him for it." His voice was as cold as ice.

"I didn't kill Soto." Padilla glanced over his shoulder like a cornered animal looking for a way out of the sealed, windowless room. "Okay, look, I tried to sell an ahayu:da, I admit it. I know it's illegal, but so what? Come on, man, they're bought and sold all the time in Santa Fe and Taos. Wise up. But I didn't take the ahayu:da from Soto—and I didn't kill him."

"If you didn't get it from Soto, then where did you get it?"

"I traded for it"

"Traded who?"

Padilla threw up his hands. "I don't know, some Indian. I met him in Taos at a meeting of the church. Sometime in late July. He said he was Zuni and claimed to be a member of one of the clans that carve the ahayu:da. The Deer Clan, or maybe the Bear Clan, I can't remember which. He never mentioned his name. And I never saw him again."

He sighed, rubbing his tired eyes with the back of his hand. Half past six, according to his watch. He hoped he had the stamina to finish what promised to be a long interrogation.

Taking a moment to gather both his thoughts and his energy, he placed the wood carving gingerly on his desk.

"Doesn't it seem odd that you and Soto were both trying to sell an ahayu:da at the same fucking time?" he asked, not bothering to hide his contempt.

Padilla glared at him.

"Two ahayu:da, imagine that. Maybe they grow on trees around here."

Antonio and Trujillo both laughed.

"Or maybe stolen ahayu:da multiply. You know, like spontaneous generation."

Padilla cringed in his chair, a look of pure hatred in his eyes. He started to say something and then changed his mind.

He continued. "Did you take the ahayu:da out of Soto's car after you killed him?"

"I didn't kill him!" Padilla shouted.

"Then did you take it out of the car after someone else killed him?" he shouted back.

Padilla shook his head.

"Let's talk about your friend John Reno. You and Reno organized the peyote meeting at your house. You and Reno organize all the meetings, as a matter of fact. So why did you tell me you didn't know him?"

Concern flashed across Padilla's face. He took a deep breath. "Because I didn't want to involve him. Why do you think? I told you, I tried to sell an ahayu:da. But I didn't kill Soto, and neither did John or any of the other church members at the meeting that night."

He rolled his eyes. "How do you know Reno?"

Padilla shrugged. "He owns a trading post in Whitewater. He's been a member of the church for about as long as I have."

"You said earlier that Reno was Road Chief. So then who were the other officials?"

"Hank and Leroy. I don't know their last names. They work for John."

"Good. Now tell me which one of you killed Soto."

Padilla muttered something under his breath. "I've already told you. A man wearing a wolf mask broke up the meeting. Soto got scared and ran away, and the man with the mask followed him. That's all I saw. That's all anyone in the teepee saw. When we heard the gunshot, Reno went out to see what happened. He came back and told us Michael was dead."

"Are you sure it was a man? Why not a wolfman? Or better yet, a skinwalker?"

Padilla looked incredulously at him, his fingers fidgeting on the table.

"What do you mean?"

"You tell me, Padilla. You do believe in skinwalkers, don't you?"

Padilla tried to stand up, but Antonio and Trujillo grabbed his arms and slammed him back down in the chair.

"Let go of me, you fucking bastards!" he screamed. Then, fighting to get his breath he sat back down in his chair and brushed the hair out of his eyes. "I want to call my lawyer. Raoul Garcia. Right now."

He smiled and stretched his arms. He took his time before continuing. "Tell me this. What if no one interrupted the peyote meeting? What if you tripped, maybe on purpose, coming into the teepee? And what if one of you put on a wolf mask and chased Soto back to his car...and killed him?"

"You're fucking crazy," Padilla shouted.

Trujillo grabbed Padilla behind the neck. "Watch your mouth, punk."

He raised his hand to stop Trujillo from getting rough.

"You know what I don't understand about you guys?" Padilla hissed. "Why you even give a shit about a sleazeball like Soto. He was just another rich gallery owner who'd sell his fucking mother for the right price. He was a thief, man. Don't you get it?"

"What? You mean he wasn't one of the People, like you and your friends?" He couldn't resist.

Padilla laughed. "One of the People?"

"Not Hispanic enough?"

"Hispanic, shit. That's a laugh. Go take another look at Soto's corpse before you bury the sonofabitch. His skin's white—and so's his money—I don't care what last name he used."

He smiled in spite of himself. So, too, did Antonio and Trujillo.

"Okay. Let's try this again. Start at the beginning and tell us everything that happened at the peyote meeting. And this time, don't leave out anything, even the smallest detail."

Disgusted, Padilla cursed in Spanish, a string of mumbled obscenities, and then began to recount the events leading up to Soto's murder.

While Padilla repeated the same bullshit story, he got up quietly from the table and excused himself, nodding for Antonio to continue. Antonio smiled, only too happy to oblige. Antonio liked Padilla even less than he did. Good luck José.

Carrying the ahayu:da in one hand and his emergency pack of cigarettes in the other, he followed the long dark hallway to the front of the station where Larry Ortega, the dispatcher on duty this evening, was brewing a fresh pot of coffee in an electric coffee maker that he stored behind the counter, off limits except for the evening shift. The aroma of the freshly brewed coffee tempted him, but he decided not to take the time to ask for a cup because he wanted to finish his work and get home as quickly as possible.

Estelle was already mad, having expressed her displeasure when he'd called earlier to tell her that, due to circumstances beyond his control, he would be late tonight, again. He always made sure to include the phrase "due to circumstances beyond my control," thinking it would lessen Estelle's anger, but somehow it never did. Nothing he could say would change her disapproval.

The last sunlight of the day flooded his office, slanting through the dirty Venetian blinds on the one window in the office with western exposure. Soon the sun would disappear behind the First Interstate Mall, plunging the office into darkness. That would mean he would have to turn on the overhead neon lights, which he hated.

He worked quickly, rummaging through the stacks of reports, notes, and Burger King napkins, looking for a slip of paper with a phone number written on it. He remembered Naranjo writing down the number at Tesuque Pueblo where he and Suino could be reached, but what had he done with it?

Eventually he found it wedged under the black desk phone along with a message slip with "Call Wanda LeClair" scribbled across it.

Wanda LeClair? It took him a moment to recall the store manager of Sabado Indian Arts who couldn't, or wouldn't, stop weeping after he told her Soto was dead. But she would have to wait until tomorrow.

When he dialed the Tesuque number, a woman answered on the first ring.

"Yes—I'm calling Robert Naranjo."

"Okay," the woman said, and then apparently set the phone down.

He heard her talking in Tewa over the muffled sounds of dishes clanking, kids crying, and dogs barking. More than a minute passed. He began to wonder if she'd forgotten him when he heard someone pick up the phone.

"Hello," came the soft voice of Naranjo.

"This is Detective Lopez calling from Santa Fe. We've arrested a man trying to sell your ahayu:da in Taos. We need you to come in and identify it. Can you stop by tomorrow morning?"

"Just a moment."

He heard the aggressive voice of Suino in the background, arguing with Naranjo. The argument lasted only a few seconds.

It was clear who won the argument when Naranjo came back on the phone. "We'll come now."

Fernando checked his watch. "Tomorrow might be better."

"No, we'd like to come now."

"Okay, suit yourself." He was not happy with this turn of events. Waiting seemed to be the theme of this long, exhausting day.

While he waited, he watched the office grow darker by increments until he could barely distinguish the framed plaques and certificates hanging on the murky walls. He found himself alone with the ahayu:da.

From its perch on his desk, Big Brother stared down at him with a dark brooding look on its mask-like face. The cylindrical woodcarving, about three feet high, appeared out of balance and ready to topple forward because of its long corkscrew-shaped umbilical cord. Underneath the umbilical cord, five parallel lines were carved into the soft wood.

The face seemed grotesque and even frightening in the half-light of the room, like a shrouded face struggling to emerge from a block of wood. He thought he detected the slight hint of a scream just below the surface of Big Brother's petrified face. Or was it only his imagination, over-stimulated by the events of this long day?

Cautiously, he reached out and touched the ahayu:da, running his hand over the smooth polished wood, and then lifted the surprisingly light figure off the desk. With Big Brother cradled in his arms, he put his feet up and closed his eyes slowly.

He dreamed of masks, wooden mask-like faces coming out of the darkness toward him, the faces changing into skinwalkers with huge red eyes and white teeth dripping blood.

When the overhead lights flashed on, his head snapped forward and his legs fell to the floor with a thud. He nearly dropped the ahayu:da as he struggled to get his balance. Though his vision was blurred, he recognized the now-familiar Nike T-shirt and Los Angeles Dodgers baseball cap

Naranjo and Suino stood awkwardly in the doorway, one of them having turned on the lights. Naranjo cleared his throat and spoke. "We came right away, like we said."

"Sure—have a seat."

He tried to regain his composure and clear his head at the same time. He replaced the ahayu:da on the desk and stood up to stretch his cramping muscles. His legs ached, and his back felt like he'd spent the entire night sleeping on a pile of rocks. Everything hurt.

Suino must have noticed his mood, because he sat down immediately and let Naranjo do the talking. The elder Zuni assumed an official bearing as he bent over the desk to examine the ahayu:da, looking closely at Big Brother's face, then at the umbilical cord and the five parallel lines below. He seemed dubious.

"What? Isn't this your ahayu:da?"

Naranjo ignored him. He picked up the woodcarving and ran his hand over the shiny white wood, turning the figure slowly in his hands. When he finished his examination, he passed the ahayu:da to Suino, who went through the same routine, except much quicker. The younger Suino did not have the older man's patience.

He could tell something was wrong by the way Suino shook his head.

"This isn't our ahayu:da,"

Fernando did not understand. "What do you mean?"

"It's a fake, a copy." Naranjo shook his head gravely, as though saddened by the sight of the counterfeit.

"How do you know it's a fake? How can you tell?"

"The finish," Naranjo said, taking the ahayu:da back from Suino. "It's too smooth. You can see where steel wool has been used, maybe even a buffing machine. Look." He held the ahayu:da for him to see.

He shrugged. He hadn't the slightest idea of what to look for.

"Not only that. See the lines here? They're not deep enough.

And the lines shouldn't be so uniform. Our carvings are not meant to be so exact."

"I'll be damned." The only thing he could think to say.

Naranjo placed the fake ahayu:da on the desk and pushed it toward him. "Whoever carved this did a professional job. Too professional."

Suino held his tongue, though he didn't bother to hide the scowl on his face.

He leaned on the desk in order to take the weight off his aching back. "What if a professional wood carver took the real ahayu:da and refinished it. Used steel wool, ran it through a buffing machine, whatever. Could it come out looking like this?"

Naranjo shook his head sadly. "It's a fake."

"Are you certain?"

"Absolutely."

He sighed, sinking back into his chair, too tired to think. Unfortunately, the two Zunis made no effort to leave. They wanted more from him.

"Has this ever happened before? Fake ahayu:da being sold on the black market?"

Naranjo was diplomatic. "Not to our knowledge."

He pondered the possibilities, all equally probable or equally improbable. Thinking about the various scenarios gave him a headache that would only get worse unless he managed to get rid of Naranjo and Suino. Quickly.

Fortunately, the two Zunis acted first. Suino walked out of the office without a word. Naranjo waited until the young man was gone, then turned to him. "We'll be at Tesuque Pueblo for another day or two. Then we'll have to go back to Zuni."

Well, thanks for coming in tonight. I'll let you know of any further developments."

Alone, he struggled to collect his thoughts. He still had to decide what to do with Padilla before calling it a day. Technically Padilla hadn't broken any laws by attempting to sell a fake ahayu:da. And as for connecting Padilla to Soto's murder, they didn't have a shred of evidence. Booking Padilla would be a waste of time. Worse, it would infuriate the District Attorney's office.

He wanted to spare himself another tongue-lashing at the hands of Steve Chabot, the D.A. from hell.

Still, he couldn't bring himself to release Padilla just yet. Not without tormenting the lying bastard a little longer.

He buzzed Larry Ortega at the front desk. "Larry, send someone back to tell Antonio to hold Padilla overnight."

Then he turned off the lights and hurried out of the office before Padilla's lawyer got wind of the situation and started to make trouble. Like everyone else.

9

He walked into the Plaza Restaurant fifteen minutes late for his lunch appointment. He hated to be late, even for a lunch with a troublemaker like Raoul Garcia, but today it couldn't be helped. They were catching hell down at the station for not making progress in the Soto investigation, so he had to spend most of the morning trying to smooth things out with the Chief and the District Attorney. He needed more time, a commodity that tended to be in short supply whenever a prominent figure in the business community fell victim to foul play. City Hall didn't give a damn about a poor working class slob, but let a Michael Soto bite the dust and watch them clamor for an arrest like a bunch of jackals. God help the unfortunate cops who failed to deliver.

The renovated version of the Plaza Restaurant bore no resemblance to the greasy spoon he remembered from his youth. Formerly a place for transients and locals to sober up in the morning, the Plaza had gone the way of most businesses in downtown Santa Fe, gone to yuppies and tourists. Not as glitzy as the Coyote Cafe and the other trendy downtown restaurants, but yuppified nonetheless. He frowned at the sight of the pastel colored walls decorated with Santa Fe posters and framed photographs of the original restaurant circa 1960.

Near the front of the restaurant a line of people stood waiting to be seated. He squeezed through the crowd and spotted Raoul schmoozing with a waitress at one of the rear tables. Raoul was a welcome sight, as much as he hated to admit it. At least they wouldn't have to wait for a table.

Raoul had called him at home earlier, while he and Estelle

were sharing a pot of coffee and a plate of fresh fruit.

Estelle had not been happy to have her breakfast interrupted.

"Lopez—we need to talk. How about lunch?" he asked right off, not being one to waste words.

"We? What do we have to talk about?"

"José Padilla."

His spirits sank as soon as he heard that name. Padilla hadn't been bluffing when he'd claimed to be represented by Raoul. Not who he wanted to deal with this morning, especially after a difficult meeting with the Chief and the District Attorney. How many tongue-lashings would he have to endure today, he wondered. He knew from years of experience that dealing with Raoul would mean only one thing—big trouble.

"Lopez!" Raoul shouted from across the room, waving him over with a pudgy hand studded with huge rings. He had known few people in his sixty years that he considered truly larger than life. Raoul was not only one of them, he was at the top of the list.

Seeing Raoul in the flesh, all 250 bloated pounds, depressed him. He remembered him as a fiery young lawyer who represented radical Chicano leaders and organizations like La Raza in the late sixties and early seventies. He called his clients "political prisoners," men and women charged with everything from growing pot to making armed raids on county courthouses. Raoul built a reputation for taking on the system every chance he got and winning more times than he lost.

Not an easy task for an aggressive, smart-ass Chicano lawyer who all the Anglos in the judicial system hated. But times had changed, and so had Raoul and his clientele. Instead of firebombing courthouses, the young Chicanos he represented now shot each other in gangs over territory or drugs, or maybe just for the pure pleasure of it. Nothing political.

And Raoul had changed, too. He continued to service his rabble-rousers, but he also did a lucrative trade in real estate development and celebrity lawsuits, having become one of the premier trial lawyers in all of northern New Mexico. There wasn't a lawyer or district attorney in the state who didn't fear coming up against Raoul. Who would have expected?

As he weaved through the closely packed tables in the

crowded restaurant, he saw Raoul smile and pass a slip of paper to the waitress.

"My man. It's been a while." Raoul shook his hand fiercely and then motioned for him to sit down.

Not long enough, he thought.

He took a seat at the table, already set for two people. He noticed Raoul really hadn't changed that much, expect for gaining fifty or so pounds around his middle.

The same black curly hair, the same drooping mustache, and the same belligerent expression. These days he wore a jacket and tie, but he made sure to undercut the professional look with jeans and snakeskin boots. But it was his bulging belly that he noticed most.

Bloated, like a stuffed sausage. Where had the Revolution gone? Too many enchiladas, that's where.

"Damn, your tie is so bright I need sunglasses to look at it."

"What...this?" the big man asked, pulling the bright yellow tie with pink polka dots out from between the table and his belly. "A sign of prosperity, *pendejo.*"

"So I hear. I haven't seen you since the Rodriguez trial."

"Poor sonofabitch. Three to five years for assaulting that bartender? It was a fucking brawl. Everybody was assaulting the bartender."

He shrugged and looked around. He didn't see any back door if he needed to step out in the alley for an emergency cigarette. It was going to be a long lunch.

"No smoking in public places," Raoul said, reading his mind. "City ordinance. They'll throw your ass in jail, Lopez. Where you been, man?"

He nodded. One thing about Raoul he didn't want to forget—he was one of the smartest motherfuckers in Santa Fe. Never underestimate the man.

When he saw the waitress coming their way, Raoul took the gum out of his mouth and stuck it up under the table. He couldn't believe his eyes. He hadn't seen anybody do that in twenty years.

"Anyway, you better stop the weeds. You look like shit."

"So everyone tells me." He was tired of hearing how bad he looked. As if Raoul looked any better.

The waitress gave them menus and glasses of water and then tossed her long black hair over her shoulder and flashed a big smile. "Can I get you guys anything to drink?"

"I'll have a Corona with extra lime." Raoul winked at the waitress. "And bring one for my compadre here, eh?"

"Just coffee, please. I'm on duty."

"Well, pardon me. You've turned in to a fucking tight-ass, Lopez."

"And you haven't slowed down a bit."

"Never." Raoul glanced quickly at the menu and then tossed it on the table. "So how you been, Lopez? I think about you sometimes. To tell you the truth, you're the only cop I like now that the bastards fired Lucian."

He laughed. "Lucian? He was caught taking brides. Red-handed."

"Details." Raoul raised his voice. "Listen, for those mercenary cocksuckers down there to accuse anyone of taking bribes is hypocritical bullshit. And you know it."

"Yeah? Since when have you become the expert on ethics?"

Ignoring him, the big man glanced around for the waitress.

"So what about you? I heard you got married last year."

Raoul laughed. "Yeah, but it didn't take. Turned out she was too young. Wanted to go dancing all the time, while I wanted to stay home and fuck. I got too much business to take care of to stay out all night long. Too hard on the old chorizo."

When the waitress appeared with their drinks, Raoul waved her over to the table as if directing traffic. "Bring it on in. Absolutely! Thank you, doll."

The waitress threw him a playful look. "Ready to order?"

"Yeah, give me the Blue Corn special, red, with a side order of posole," Raoul said.

He nodded. "I'll have the same."

She wrote down their orders and then, still smiling at Raoul, bounced away.

He couldn't resist asking. "Do you know her?"

"Rosalie? Sure, she's my ex-wife's little sister." He dropped a slice of green lime into his Corona. After a long drink of beer, he wiped a layer of white foam from his black mustache and grinned. "I think I married the wrong woman."

"Small world."

"Absolutely. That's why I called you, Lopez. Because it's a small world."

Raoul paused for effect, but he ignored the theatrics. "Stop the bullshit, Raoul. What do you want?"

"Hey, don't get all bent out of shape. I already said you're the only cop I like. Lighten up, for Christ's sake."

They glared at each other.

"Okay...what I want is José Padilla," Raoul said sharply. "When are you going to release him?"

"We haven't decided."

"Your twenty-four hours are up, man."

"Not quite."

"You got nothing on him, Lopez. Nada. Why hold him if you can't find a charge that'll stick?"

Sighing, he dumped sugar and cream into his coffee and then carefully stirred it. "That's our decision. We'll make it as soon as we can. You know how the system works."

"Fuck the system. You don't have one shred of evidence to connect José to Michael Soto's murder. You got nothing. So why do you want to harass him?"

"He's lying. And you know it as well as I do."

"Lying? What the fuck does that mean? Who's not lying? The point is, you don't have a reason to hold my client in your jail."

He laughed. "How about a dead body in his front yard? That's not reason enough?"

"Come on, man, there was a fucking meeting of the Native American Church on José's property that night. We're talking about a peyote ceremony. You know how long those things last."

He corrected Raoul. "The meeting ended at midnight. Padilla didn't call us until eight in the morning."

"So what? They were stoned on peyote. It fucks up your sense of time. You know that as well as I do."

"How convenient."

Raoul stopped his harangue while Rosalie delivered his Blue

Corn special and posole. "Thanks, doll," he said tersely, no longer smiling.

He started on his enchiladas, but Raoul kept staring, not finished.

"Tell me, why do you cops always pick on small guys like José?" Garcia asked finally. "I mean, he's an *enjarrador*, for Christ's sake. A plasterer. Why pick on the little guys all the time? Why not go after the big fish?"

"Like who?"

"Like Michael Soto. Do you know how much profit he turned on his black market bullshit? Do you have any fucking idea?"

He paused between bites of posole. "Only one problem with that, Raoul. Soto's dead."

Garcia grabbed a flour tortilla, dipped it in his posole, and bit off the end. "You had all summer to nail the sleazy bastard. Everyone in Santa Fe knew what kind of business Soto was running. It wasn't turquoise trinkets, pal."

Coming here had been a terrible mistake, he realized. He ignored Raoul for the moment and instead tried to finish his lunch as quickly as possible so that he could get the hell out of here.

"Do you understand what I'm saying?" Raoul demanded, an incendiary note in his voice. "You work for the *man*, and you don't even know it. Look around you, Lopez. Who's the chief of police? Larry Stuart. Who's the prosecutor? Steve Chabot. Who's the mayor? Clyde Wetterman. All of them are Anglos, in case you haven't noticed. They've got you by the *cojones*, you and all the other whitewashed Chicano cops who sold out to the system for a few fucking dollars a month to pay the rent and keep the old lady and the kids happy."

"Wait a minute. Don't give me that tired shit about the People. Fuck the People. Soto was just as Hispanic as José Padilla."

"What?" Raoul nearly choked on his food. "You're fucking crazy. If Soto was Hispanic, it was in name only."

"There's more to it than that." He shook his head angrily, his hands shaking on the table. "Listen, not everything comes down to a question of race. It's not Us against Them in every goddamn thing we do. Maybe I thought that once, when I was younger, but

I don't believe it any more. Telling the good guys from the bad just isn't that fucking simple."

Now that he had Raoul's attention, he moderated his voice. "What you say about city hall is true, at least for the moment. But we've had Chicano mayors, and we'll have them again. And as for sleazeballs, what's the difference between a Chicano who steals a sacred communal object and a Chicano—or Anglo—gallery owner who sells it on the black market? What's the difference between Padilla and Soto? Tell me?"

"Money. Padilla needs the money."

"Hah! So money's the only difference? But Soto thought he needed the money, too. Every sonofabitch in the city thinks he needs more money."

"So what are you saying?"

"Just this, that everything doesn't come down to a question of race. You can't see every issue as racial, and you can't settle every dispute by dividing up according to race. Life's not that fucking simple. If it were, Indians wouldn't murder Indians, and Anglos wouldn't murder Anglos. Who knows, two Chicanos like us might even be able to get along."

"Yeah, but I'm talking about exploitation."

"So am I," he replied. "It happened—it still happens. I don't deny it. But exploitation doesn't always mean one race exploiting another. Sometimes people use race to hide behind—as a way of distracting attention from the real issue. The problem usually comes down to people fucking over people."

Suddenly Raoul burst out laughing. "Jesus, Fernando, you've turned into some kind of reactionary preacher."

"Old age, I guess."

Raoul pushed away his plate and swilled the last of his Corona. "Not a bad meal." He patted his big stomach. "Red chile could be hotter, but what else is new, eh?"

Raoul belched, excused himself, and then leaned over the table toward him. "So what about José?"

"What about him?"

"You're right, he's a fucking pain in the ass. But he's not a murderer, he's just a poor slob trying to scrape together a living. You know the story."

"Yeah, I know. We'll release him this afternoon. Unless something turns up, which I doubt. So tell me this, what the hell was he doing trying to sell a fake ahayu:da? Where did he get it?"

Raoul shook his head in disgust. "Soto, where do you think? I tried to warn him, but you know how he is. Like talking to a fucking rock."

"Do you know for a fact that he got it from Soto?"

"Where else would he get it?"

He tossed his napkin on the table and took out his Camel Lights. Then, remembering, he put the cigarettes back in his shirt pocket and frowned. "Well, you better talk to Padilla. Maybe he'll listen to you now. The man definitely has an attitude problem."

The big man laughed. "Tell me about it."

When the check came, Raoul opened his wallet and slapped a fifty dollar bill on the table. "Keep the change, doll. Let's get together sometime, just you and me. Maybe go to El Farol for a drink. What do you say?"

Laughing, Rosalie snatched the money and disappeared.

Raoul slapped him on the back. "You see, I married the wrong woman."

He followed Raoul to the door. On their way out they met a group of three noisy young men coming into the restaurant talking and laughing. Raoul broke out in a big smile when he saw them and raised his hand to give high fives all around.

"Hey, Paul. Where you been, man?" he asked the youngest of the three, a short wiry Chicano wearing jeans, a black T-shirt, and a red bandana tied around his neck.

Paul patted his stomach. "I see where you've been, Raoul."

Raoul chuckled. "Too much red chile, bro."

The three young men laughed.

Raoul turned to him and pointed proudly at Paul. "This is my kid brother, Paul. My famous kid brother. He won second prize at the Spanish Market last month for one of his santos. Big fucking deal. Now he can raise his prices, eh Paul?" he asked, punching his brother in the shoulder.

"All these guys belong to the same society in Chimayo, Santeros Artesana. I wouldn't trust any of them. Bunch of fucking drunks. Including my brother."

He nodded awkwardly, not interested in the Garcia family jokes.

"Remember what I said, I'll be coming up to see you this weekend."

Paul laughed. "Thanks for the warning. We'll hide the Corona."

While they traded jokes, he seized the opportunity to escape. He shook Raoul's hand and then turned to the three santeros. "Nice to meet you."

Once free of the Garcia brothers, he walked down Lincoln Avenue, avoiding the Plaza. Jaywalking, he dodged the Roadrunner tour bus, a goofy oversized golf cart with bright red road runners painted on its sides, and then walked past the Museum of Fine Arts and cut up to Washington Avenue. By the time he crossed Washington to the municipal parking lot, he'd almost washed away the memory of Raoul's radical Chicano act, his bullshit politics.

Almost, but not quite. His accusations, like Padilla's earlier, left a bitter taste in his mouth, a sour unsettled feeling that kept him on edge.

Seeing Antonio and Fidel huddled together talking in the parking lot took his mind off Raoul. As he approached, Antonio turned to face him.

"Have you seen the newspaper?"

He shook his head. "Why?"

Fidel explained. "We did a story on Michael Soto's will. Apparently Soto left everything to Wanda LeClair. That's according to the will Raoul Garcia filed in Probate Court."

He shook his head. "Wanda LeClair, eh? How cozy."

"Too cozy," Antonio said.

Fidel leaned closer. "That's not all. We're running a follow-up tomorrow, because we found out Soto's will was witnessed by none other than your friend José Padilla."

"No kidding?"

"So what do you know about Wanda LeClair?

"Who is she?" Antonio asked.

He smiled. "She may be our wild card. The missing link."

10

He paced back and forth in his office, furious. He'd just stormed out of Larry Stuart's office, after being read the riot act by the Chief for failing to produce results in the Soto investigation. Why hadn't they found Soto's killer? What was taking so long? He could still hear Stuart's insulting voice:

"We're not talking about some two-bit pottery importer on Cerrillos Road, we're talking about Michael Soto, the owner of Sabado Indian Arts on the fucking Plaza. We can't let some sonofabitch shoot him like a dog out in Jaconita and not make an arrest. It makes all of us look bad. Do you understand?"

He understood only too well. The business community and the Chamber of Commerce types were putting pressure on Stuart and District Attorney Steve Chabot. They wanted an arrest, a quick resolution. Soto may have been a newcomer to their club, but he was one of theirs nonetheless. Unseemly things like this just didn't happen to powerful people like them, people who owned shops and galleries on the famous Santa Fe Plaza.

Problem was, he didn't have a case yet. Too many leads, too many questions yet to be answered. So he had asked for more time, just a few days.

Stuart's face had turned red. "You came in yesterday with the same fucking story. Look at the facts. Michael Soto turns up dead in José Padilla's front yard. Padilla gets arrested trying to sell a Zuni tribal object, or a fake Zuni tribal object, that may or may not have belonged to Soto. Then our man Padilla turns up as witness to a will naming Soto's gallery manager, Wanda LeClair, as executor and beneficiary of Soto's entire estate. Not to mention the fact that Wanda LeClair's lawyer, Raoul Garcia, just happens to represent José Padilla. Now I ask you, how can it be so fucking hard to get the goods on these people?"

That was all he could take. He'd stormed out of Stuart's office, slamming the door behind him. Fuck Stewart. Fuck Chabot. He was doing the best he could. What did the bastards want from him anyway?

There had been bad blood between him and the Chief for years. As a consequence he had a reputation for being prickly. But who wouldn't be after watching one Anglo after another being promoted ahead of him. It took him twenty years to make detective. Compare that to the five years it took the chief's nephew to make detective. What a joke. Dickless Andy as the other cops called him had the lightest workload of any of them.

Even worse, he got it from both sides of the spectrum. To the Anglos, he was a Chicano with an attitude. To the La Raza agitators and hotheads, he had sold out his own people to work for the Man. He'd set himself against the People.

Well, fuck all of them. He just wanted to do his fucking job without being harassed. Call him old fashioned, he happened to believe that murderers and other scumbags should be off the streets.

Back in his office he began pacing, too agitated to sit down. He nearly exploded when he saw Stuart standing in his doorway, following him.

"Listen...Fernando...you're a good cop. I want you to know we appreciate the work you do," said Stuart tentatively, trying to gloss over their differences. He was a small clean-cut man with wire-rimmed glasses and moussed hair, all of forty years old.

"Just try to understand my position. I'm getting calls from the mayor, from the Chamber of Commerce, from the Downtown Realtor's Association. I'm even getting calls from gallery owners as far away as Taos, and all of them want to know why the fuck we can't find Michael Soto's murderer. What am I supposed to tell them?"

"Tell them the investigation will be complete in forty-eight hours."

That turned out to be a mistake, because Stuart had called

him on his vague promise. If he couldn't bring a chargeable case to the prosecutor's office within forty-eight hours, then Stuart would turn the investigation over to one of the younger detectives, either Manny or Armando.

Thinking about the possibility of Stuart giving the case to Manny or Armando made him even angrier. Manny was more of a computer, data-base kind of guy. Armando was the youngest detective on the force, thirty-five years old and still wet behind the ears.

Something had to give today, or one of them would get to finish the investigation—and get all the credit. He couldn't let that happen. He'd resign or take early retirement before letting Stuart give the case to Manny or Armando. Maybe this would be the excuse he needed.

No time for another cup of coffee today. He needed to get off his ass and talk to Wanda LeClair. Not to mention John Reno. He'd postponed the drive to Whitewater long enough. Too long. Maybe that had been his mistake. He'd given all the players too much rope. Well, round-up time had come, ladies and gentlemen.

He looked around his office for the fake ahayu:da, then remembered he'd put it in the closet with his supply of clean shirts and all the other junk he didn't know what to do with. He found it on the floor of the closet, perched on top of a box of old records that someone had decided to store in his closet years ago and then forgotten about. Bringing the ahayu:da back with him, he cleared a space for it on his desk and then sat down facing the mysterious woodcarving whose elongated face looked down at him.

He felt again the smoothness of the wood, the long thin nose and the outline of the lower jaw, which dropped halfway to the umbilical cord. The smoothness reminded him of Naranjo's comment—the fake ahayu:da had been professionally finished, perhaps with a buffing machine. Even the edges felt uniformly smooth to his fingertips.

Someone knocked on the door, interrupting his reveries. He hoped it wasn't the chief coming to tell him he'd changed his mind and had decided to give the Soto case to Manny or Armando immediately. What a relief to see Antonio.

"The reports you wanted." Antonio waved the papers at Fernando.

"Bueno."

Antonio nodded toward the ahayu:da. "Damn, I see why they call it a war god. That's a mean looking piece of wood, especially with the billy-club sticking out like that."

He laughed. "The billy-club? It really does look more like a penis than an umbilical cord, doesn't it?

He grabbed the ahayu:da and placed it on the floor behind his desk where it wouldn't distract them.

Antonio cleared his throat. "Okay, I have reports on both Wanda LeClair and Jose Padilla. LeClair, age thirty-two, single, Anglo. She's originally from San Diego, where her father was in the Navy and her mother worked at the base. She was romantically involved with Soto. In fact, they were living together in his room at La Fonda. She had been an associate professor of cultural anthropology at the University of New Mexico until she resigned last year to manage Sabado Indian Arts. No prior record, except for a couple of arrests for disorderly conduct while a student at San Diego State University. Demonstrations, political marches that turned disorderly. Both times the charges were dropped. Her colleagues at UNM said she was a loner, not very friendly. Her department voted to give her tenure two years ago, but the vote was close, fourteen to eleven."

"What's tenure?"

"Means she has a permanent job. She goes from assistant to associate professor."

He nodded. "So why would she leave a tenured position at UNM to manage a gallery?"

The question hung in the air for several seconds.

Antonio shook his head. "Love? Money?"

"Could be. UNM's salaries are notoriously low."

"Sure." Antonio approached his desk. "That makes sense. I mean, she's a cultural anthropologist interested in Indian artifacts. Maybe she decided she could make more money selling stolen Indian artifacts than teaching. We know she and Soto were working together. Hell, maybe she has the real ahayu:da as we speak. Maybe she's trying to sell it right now."

He pondered the possibility that she had the ahayu:da. The idea of a former professor selling a stolen tribal object on the black market seemed a bit far-fetched. No doubt professors at UNM needed money like all other employees of the state of New Mexico, but surely a tenured professor like her could find easier ways to supplement her income. Then again, what better leads did they have at the moment?

"The LeClair woman has to be involved."

"I don't know, Antonio. It doesn't feel right to me. I can't decide what to make of her."

Antonio shuffled the papers in his big hands. "Okay, second report. José Padilla. We already have most of this information. He's fifty years old, widowed, Chicano. His wife died three years ago of breast cancer. Two sons, one in the Army, stationed in Germany, and the other works for the National Forest Service in Jémez Springs. He calls himself an *enjarrador,* a plasterer specializing in adobe fireplaces and mud stucco. But he does odd jobs, too. Some carpentry. Even some construction work when he needs the money. Sounds like he was more prosperous a few years back. He made handcrafted furniture in the early two thousands. Taos sofas, coffee tables with Indian designs, that kind of thing. When he got tired of making furniture, he joined a group of artisans in Chimayo called Santeros Artesana carving santos, bultos, and retablos. That lasted three or four years. Since then he's been a laborer, basically."

He nodded, then scratched the stubble on his chin, noticing how poorly he had shaved that morning.

Antonio continued. "According to his neighbors in Jaconita, he keeps to himself most of the time. "They say he's been depressed since his wife died. Down on his luck. His nearest neighbors, Felix Sanchez and his wife, claim they haven't seen him around much for the past few months. And they both should know, since Felix is retired and the both of them are home every day—"

"Wait a minute," he said, raising his hand. "What did you say about the group of artisans in Chimayo? What was the name?"

"Santeros Artesana. Padilla worked with them for three or four years."

"That's it!" he said loudly, startling Antonio, who glanced

down at the papers in his hands, looking for what he'd missed.

"What?"

"Finally, a connection."

"I don't follow you."

He picked up the ahayu:da and placed it back on the desk, turning the tall woodcarving so that it faced Antonio. "Don't you see, Padilla or one of the others carved this fake ahayu:da at Santeros Artesana and then tried to sell it in Taos. He copied the original, the one stolen from Zuni this summer—or maybe he gave it to another of the santeros to copy. Either way he had a hand in the deception."

"How do you know?"

He smiled. "Because Padilla's lawyer, Raoul Garcia, has a younger brother who's a member of Santeros Artesana. That explains why Garcia represented Padilla even before Padilla needed a lawyer. And the will. They must be working together."

Antonio nodded. "And what about Garcia's other client, Wanda LeClair?"

"Absolutely."

He remembered the theatrics of the weeping woman in Sabado Indian Arts. Was her grief genuine, or was it only a performance? She had played her cards well, played them well enough to get control of Soto's gallery and everything else the man owned—if, that is, the will she and Raoul had produced stood up in Probate Court.

But there was an even bigger question—did their plans to take control of Sabado Indian Arts include killing Soto?

"Let's go," he said to Antonio.

"Chimayo?"

"That's our first stop," he said.

11

Below the hand-painted "Santeros Artesana" sign hung a steer skull with black horns. The empty eye sockets stared in his general direction as he pulled into the gravel parking lot behind two half-ton pickups and a beat-up 1956 Chevy. His old Plymouth Acclaim belched once and then gave up the ghost with one last furious rattle.

"I hope this damn things starts again."

He ignored Antonio's comment, focusing instead on the intricately carved death figure, Doña Sebastiana. Old lady death sat atop a miniature ox cart protecting the front door of Santeros Artesana. Though the mythical Doña Sebastiana remained a favorite of Spanish artisans, especially in old Penitente villages like Chimayo, this rendition struck him as something special.

The carved bones of the skeleton seemed to flow together, as sensual as the delicate limbs of an adolescent child budding into puberty. Sitting in the ox cart with her arms resting on bent knees, Doña Sebastiana appeared without her traditional bow and arrow. Instead, she cradled in her hands the rather macabre offering of a detached skull. The ox cart itself had been constructed of cedar branches stacked like toothpicks and then tied together with twine, propped up on a wooden axle and wheels carved from cottonwood stumps. The skull in Doña Sebastiana's hands looked perfectly real to him, too real for comfort.

Not ten feet behind Doña Sebastiana a screen door painted bright turquoise stood in stark contrast to the grisly reminders of death that together seemed to guard the entrance to Santeros

Artesana. A cheerful place, he thought, as he climbed out of the Plymouth and stretched his cramped legs.

Down the dirt road leading to the *santuario* a pack of dogs howled forlornly in the still, hot morning. Already scorching, the sun burned down on the Plymouth, reflecting off the patches of gray primer beneath the fading paint. He dropped his sunglasses into his shirt pocket and headed for the door, careful to avoid the sadistic smile of Doña Sebastiana who, with her ox cart, stood ready to gather lost souls.

Opening the screen door, he found the inside door made of steel. And locked. He pounded on the door, waiting for someone to answer. He could hear noises inside, but no one seemed to be in any hurry to open the door. He pounded again, this time louder.

Finally the door opened a crack and he found himself staring at Paul Garcia looking exactly the same as when big brother Raoul had introduced him outside the Plaza Restaurant. Jeans, black T-shirt, and a dirty red bandana tied loosely around his neck. "Yeah? What do you want?"

"Police. Open the door, we need to ask you a few questions." He showed his badge.

"We're closed," the kid said and tried to close the door.

"Not so fast." He pushed the door open with his shoulder sending Garcia reeling backward.

"You can't come in here. You need a fucking warrant."

"Antonio, show him the warrant."

He stepped past Garcia into the building, noticing how the unplastered walls of the L-shaped adobe revealed the individual adobe bricks, exposed and already disintegrating even though the building couldn't be more than ten years old. Looked like Santeros Artesana should pay more attention to plastering and less attention to graveyard décor.

As Antonio stepped forward and unfolded the warrant, he heard footsteps off to the left and the sound of a door slamming shut.

Garcia's mouth fell open as if to speak, but instead he stood back against the wall, unsure of himself.

He paused a moment to survey the lay of the house. The front door opened into a tiny office, almost as cluttered as his, with what appeared to be a living area to the right. To the left he saw a long room running perpendicular to the rest of the house, most of it out of sight from where he stood. The big room served as their workshop. He could tell by the layer of blond wood chips littering the floor.

Garcia quickly managed to regain his composure and his mouth. "What do you want? Why are you harassing us?" He tried to block them from entering the workshop area.

"Stand back, please."

"Do you know who my brother is?" Garcia's baby face broke into a smirk. "He's a big time lawyer—"

He cut off Garcia. "Yeah, I had lunch with him yesterday."

"You." The kid seemed to recognize him now. "Then why are you harassing us if you're a friend of my brother's?"

He smiled. "I didn't say I was a friend. Now get out of my way."

When he brushed past, Garcia jumped back and yelped like a wounded puppy, fear getting the better of him. The kid was strung too tight for the kind of role he had chosen to play.

Antonio, scowling, followed behind him and further intimidated Garcia who lost his balance and stumbled backward into a gray metal desk facing the entrance.

He followed a trail of fresh wood chips into the workshop and found two other men sitting on metal folding chairs pretending to be working on carvings they held in their laps. Ignoring the scene at the front door, they continued to chisel and scrape as though nothing had happened. Just another day at the office. Bad acting, all the way around.

He recognized the younger of the two as one of Garcia's companions at the Plaza Restaurant. The other one looked to be in his mid-fifties with a bushy gray mustache and a big belly spilling out of his white T-shirt and over the top of his khaki chinos.

Old enough to be the father of Garcia or the other kid.

"Police."

The older man stopped carving and looked at him but said nothing.

When the man didn't respond, he took the opportunity to look around the room. It wasn't exactly a workshop, but a converted living room still furnished with a sofa and several wooden tables that served as workbenches, cluttered with knives and chisels and small woodworking tools.

One round table near a bulky wood-burning stove along the rear wall provided space for a collection of unfinished carvings, all of them fashioned from the same soft blond wood, either cottonwood or aspen. He saw both santos and bultos, three-dimensional carvings of various saints, as well as the bas relief carvings known as retablos.

On another table closer to the front stood an arrangement of finished pieces—statues of St. Francis and St. James and a host of other saints whose names he could no longer remember. Intricately carved and brightly painted, the statuary seemed more dramatic and compelling than the retablos hanging on the wall above the table. He especially noticed a bulto of St. James, or Santiago as he was called in Northern New Mexico, riding on his prancing white steed with sword in hand and a stern militaristic smile fixed on his face.

"What are you looking for?" the older man asked, interrupting his thoughts.

For the moment he chose to ignore the question, admiring the quality of the work displayed on the table.

Clearly, the members of Santeros Artesana were accomplished craftsmen—hadn't Raoul Garcia bragged that his brother had won second prize at this summer's Spanish Market? So then why would they get involved in a scheme to carve a fake ahayu:da and sell it on the black market? The question saddened him, because he already knew the answer.

"Don't tell them anything." Garcia spoke from the doorway, carefully stepping around Antonio, who stood at the front of the room with his hands planted firmly on his hips, daring anyone to misbehave.

"I haven't asked any questions yet."

As he walked across the floor, he heard the wood chips crunch under his shoes. He approached the kid who gripped a small knife tightly in the palm of his hand, as if trying to decide what to do with it. He motioned toward the carving on the kid's lap. "Nice work."

The kid was silent.

Enjoying himself, he turned to the older man, who sat in a chair blocking the door to what looked like a small closet. "Move your chair, please."

The man did as he was told.

He found the door locked. "Where's the key?" When the older man didn't respond, he turned to the kid.

Antonio broke the silence. "Open the fucking door, or I'll break it down! He moved toward the closet door.

The older man held up his hand. "Wait. This is my house." He reached into his pocket for the key.

He inserted the key and opened the door, not surprised to find a closet filled with supplies. Cardboard boxes containing paints and wood stains occupied most of the floor space. Unpeeled cottonwood and aspen logs, cut in two- to three-foot lengths, were stacked on the two overhead shelves, both of which sagged under the weight of the wood. Then something else caught his eye. It was tucked behind a box of wood stain, wrapped in a white sheet. He squatted on the floor and reached in for the bundle. Light as a feather. Just as he expected it would be.

Carrying the bundle to the nearest table, he brushed aside an assortment of empty beer cans and woodworking tools in order to make room, the falling objects echoing loudly in the silent room. He unwrapped the sheet carefully, not wanting to damage the contents.

"Take a look." He called over Antonio.

Antonio looked at the two carvings and smiled.

"The stolen ahayu:da, I assume." He ran his fingers over the rough wood of the first piece.

The second piece was a half-finished ahayu:da, with only the elongated face emerging out of the block of new blond wood. A copy, another fake, like the one José Padilla had tried to sell in Taos. Except this one would never be finished.

"Did Soto give you the original to copy?" he asked, his eyes moving from one frightened face to another. "Or did you kill Soto to get it?"

"You're crazy. Soto brought it to us." The kid sounded worried now.

Garcia intervened. "Shut up. Don't tell them anything. We're not answering any questions until we talk to our lawyer."

He smiled. "Your brother, you mean."

"Fuck you!" Garcia hissed.

"Yeah, yeah, don't waste my time, kid. Go on, sit down over there until we're finished. You understand?"

Garcia started to mouth off again, but when Antonio stepped in front of him he thought twice about it and took a seat by his young friend. The older man lowered his head and began to rub his forehead.

Meanwhile, he wrapped the two woodcarvings in the sheet and then turned to Antonio. "Go call Tomas Trujillo and tell him to get up to Chimayo as fast as he can. I want him to finish here."

While Antonio went to call Trujillo, he took an empty chair and waited. He desperately wanted a cigarette but decided against it. Too many wood chips on the floor. Too many chemicals.

Antonio reappeared in the doorway. "He's on his way."

"Good. Keep our friends company while I look around the office."

"When do I get to call my lawyer?" Garcia asked.

"Soon." He turned his back and walked into the tiny office. He squeezed between the file cabinet and the corner of the desk so that he could sit in the cushioned office chair.

The clutter of papers on the desk made him feel right at home. Except there wasn't enough room for him to push back his chair and put his feet on the desk. What a pity, he decided, as he leafed through a plastic tray piled high with bills, receipts, and purchase orders. No organization whatsoever.

He leaned back in the chair and surveyed the Spanish Market posters tacked along the front wall. Another poster, mounted and framed in black aluminum, hung on the wall beside the desk, just above a small computer table, where an old PC and a cheap Panasonic printer collected dust. The poster, from Santa Fe's Museum of International Folk Art, showed a collection of antique dolls all crunched together for a group photograph. The dark, pinched little faces looked grotesque, he thought. He couldn't decide if the problem was poor lighting or the dreary Victorian clothing of the dolls, shades of dull red and gloomy brown.

Then he noticed a wastebasket below the computer table, a brown wicker basket that looked like it hadn't been emptied in weeks. Papers and half-filled Coors cans spilled out onto the floor in a soggy puddle of trash. He resisted the urge to examine the trash until he saw the Sabado Indian Arts business envelope, ripped open at one end. At first he carefully sifted through the refuse, then lost his patience and poured the whole damn basket out on the floor, banana peels, apple cores, wads of chewing gum and all. Using his shoe, he pushed the trash around on the tile floor, looking for what had been inside the Sabado envelope.

Whatever it was, he didn't find it.

He was ready to call it quits when he noticed what looked like a draft of a short letter, crumpled and apparently discarded because of several typos underlined and corrected in black ink. He unfolded the letter and read: "If you want the real ahayu:da, go see Michael Soto, the owner of Sabado Indian Arts gallery in Santa Fe. Soto is trying to sell the ahayu:da for $50,000." Signed "A friend," the letter was addressed to none other than John Reno, Whitewater Zuni Traders, Whitewater, New Mexico. Almost word for word the same letter Naranjo and Suino had shown him in his office.

Santeros Artesana had sent the letters.

One to the Zuni Tribal Council, and one to John Reno.

Smiling, he folded the letter and tucked it in his shirt pocket. Maybe, just maybe, he might make the forty-eight-hour deadline the chief had given him. Let them try to take the investigation away from him now. He was too close to finding Soto's killer. They wouldn't dare.

From outside came the distant wail of sirens. He listened as the sirens grew louder, approaching from the direction of the *santuario*. Finally he heard the sirens turn onto the dirt road leading to Santeros Artesana and scream to a stop.

"Fuck!" Antonio cursed from the next room.

Only a cop as juvenile as Trujillo would insist on such an overly dramatic entrance. He searched for just the right word to characterize Trujillo. Juvenile didn't even begin to do him justice.

"What's the crazy bastard doing?" Antonio asked from the doorway.

He shrugged. Crazy bastard sounded good. Better than juvenile.

He walked outside into the disapproving glare of Doña Sebastiana. Seen from the side, old lady death seemed to be laughing at the skull she held in her hands. Got you. Either that or she was proudly displaying her catch as a reminder to the briefly living of what they could look forward to in the future. All life-roads led inevitably to Doña Sebastiana.

Strange sense of humor, he thought as he walked to the parking lot just in time to watch Trujillo and three other deputies pile recklessly out of their two squad cars as though acting in some low budget TV cop show.

"Thanks for the audience." He pointed down the road to the village where a group of curious onlookers had collected near the *santuario*, peering at them through a thick cloud of red dust.

"What?" Trujillo smiled, oblivious to his comment. "Did you find Soto's killer here?"

"Not yet." He did his best to explain the situation quickly, without getting bogged down in too many details.

Trujillo listened quietly. "So these guys had the real ahayu:da? And they were making copies to sell?"

"Exactly. So here's what I want you to do, Tomas. Read them their rights and then take the three of them to Santa Fe and hold them until I get back later today. Understand?"

Trujillo nodded.

"And Tomas, find the other members of Santeros Artesana. I know there's a least one more, a kid about Paul Garcia's age. Early twenties."

"No problem."

He watched as Trujillo and his deputies entered the building.

Moments later Antonio came out of the building carrying the two ahayu:da wrapped loosely in their white sheet. He opened the trunk of the Plymouth and stood back while Antonio deposited the bundle next to the spare tire.

He paused for a moment before closing the trunk in order to offer an apology to the ahayu:da. Better to be safe than sorry.

"Forgive me for the inconvenience—but please, no earthquakes or natural disasters."

Then he slammed the trunk closed and dusted off his hands.

Finally he turned to Antonio and grabbed the big man's shoulder. "Time's running out. We need to work fast. I'll drive. You call the Station. Have them check Sabado Indian Arts. If Wanda LeClair isn't there, then I want them to put out an all-points bulletin."

"Where are we going?" Antonio headed for the passenger's seat.

"Here." He took the letter out of his shirt pocket and handed it to Antonio over the roof of the car.

12

Sitting stiffly at the counter of the Dixie Diner, he hunched his shoulders and munched, delicately, on his grilled cheese sandwich. Antonio had given up on his lunch, a blackened Reuben that lay half-eaten on its plastic plate. The big man was still pissed at his decision to stop for lunch at the truck stop on I-40 just west of Albuquerque. Why take the time? Who needs lunch?

Antonio glanced at their check and then passed it on to him.

"My pleasure." He followed Antonio to the cashier, a thin blonde with ratted hair and bright red lipstick who looked forty but was probably closer to thirty.

The woman smiled. "How was everything?"

"Just fine." He ignored Antonio, who hovered at the door anxious to get going. Antonio couldn't stay still, not for one moment. He was a human perpetual motion machine.

After going back to the counter to leave a tip for the waitress, he joined Antonio outside in the noisy parking lot, crowded with cars, vans, and RVs. The truck stop stank of diesel fuel and burnt rubber, while traffic roared by on the interstate. To the east, just beyond the diesel pumps, rows of semi-trailers blocked what would have been a spectacular view of Albuquerque sprawled at the foot of the Sandia Mountains.

"Here, you drive for a while." He tossed the keys to Antonio.

Glad for the opportunity to stay busy, Antonio climbed into the Plymouth and began adjusting the front seat and rearview mirror. All business now, he started the engine and carefully backed out of the parking space, then put the Plymouth in gear and headed for the on-ramp.

He marveled at the intensity and dedication with which Antonio drove, both hands placed firmly on the steering wheel in the recommended two and ten o'clock positions.

Such precision puzzled him. He normally drove with one hand, leaving the other free to fumble with his pack of cigarettes, cup of coffee, or whatever. Not that he considered himself a careless driver, far from it. He liked to think of his driving as uninhibited.

"Something wrong?"

He realized he'd been staring. He opened the glove compartment to get a New Mexico road map. "No, nothing's wrong."

"Do you know where we're going?"

"I will in a second."

He divided his attention between the map and the flat-topped mesas to the north of I-40. He noticed a nasty wind kicking up from the southwest, blowing dust and dead tumbleweeds across the highway and into the ditch, where they stuck in the barbed wire fences. Perhaps a late summer storm, coming up from the Gulf of California, though he saw no threatening clouds in the sky. Only a few high cirrus clouds, casting dark fleeting shadows on the highway ahead of them and the sagebrush flats to either side.

The wind reminded him of early spring, when dust devils and blowing tumbleweed could come up suddenly, blinding even the most experienced driver. He wondered what Antonio would do in such a situation. Did he have dust devils figured out, too? Off in the distance he noticed Laguna Pueblo, situated on its barren rock, with the blue shadow of Mount Taylor looming behind it further to the north. He hadn't been down here in many years—the land looked even drier than he remembered.

The dusty adobes of Laguna spilled down the hill from the summit, where the whitewashed San José de Laguna Church overlooked the sprawling pueblo. Only the green willows and tamarisks growing along the banks of the San José River at the base of the pueblo seemed cool, offering shade and water to the children he saw playing in the river. It was a dry, harsh land where water had always been the most precious commodity.

How strange to think the early Spanish explorers, seeing Laguna and the other pueblos for the first time, thought they'd found the mythical Seven Cities of Gold, sometimes called Cibola or Quivera. The Spanish obsession with the Seven Cities of Gold had always confounded him. What folly. He shifted uncomfortably on the seat. "What do you think? Does Laguna look like a city of gold?"

"What? Are you crazy?" Antonio did not take his eyes off the highway.

He sighed. "Just thinking to myself."

Near the exit to Acoma, he decided to rest his eyes. He leaned his head back on the seat and tried to empty his mind of all thought, exactly like Estelle told him to do when insomnia kept him awake at night. He couldn't seem to distance himself from work, couldn't find the psychic space necessary to relax. Instead, he worried about all the problems of all the people who came to him. It was not a healthy habit, he knew.

He opened his eyes when he felt the Plymouth begin to slow down.

"We need gas. You should have told me back in Albuquerque."

He shrugged and then checked his watch. Just after two o'clock. They would get to Whitewater in plenty of time.

Antonio turned off the interstate and pulled into a Sunoco station. He stopped beside a self-service pump. "You want to do it?"

"Go ahead. I have to take a leak."

When he got back to the car, Antonio was talking on the radio. "Okay...we'll check it out," Antonio said, signing off.

He climbed into the passenger's seat and slammed the car door.

Not wasting any time, Antonio revved the engine and headed back to the interstate. "It's the LeClair woman."

"What about her?"

"You were right, she's running. They found her car at the mission church in Zuni. Abandoned, it looks like. The Tribal Police reported it a short time ago and called in the highway patrol to do a license check."

He frowned. "Damn. What's her role in all this?"

"I was thinking—"

"Thinking what? Jesus Christ, finish your sentence."

"Maybe she's the supplier, the connection we've been looking for. You know, since she's an anthropologist, she could have access to tribal objects like the ahayu:da. Maybe she stole it, or arranged to have it stolen. Maybe she and Soto worked together. As a team."

Brooding, he closed his eyes again and meditated on Wanda LeClair. This was a further complication.

"I wonder. Soto worked with Reno. He got his black market goods at the peyote meetings. Some of them anyway."

"Then where does Wanda LeClair come in?"

He shook his head, stuffing the road map back into the glove compartment, and then pointed to the Interstate sign for Highway 53. "Take the back road to Zuni. It's faster. We'll stop at the pueblo, take a look at LeClair's car, and then go on to Whitewater."

Antonio did as he was told, pushing the Plymouth up to seventy-five on the deserted highway, speeding through the black lava rock formations of the Malpais and past the rocky summit of Inscription Rock. Only when they entered the city limits of Ramah did Antonio slow down, and then only for the few seconds it took to drive through the scattering of cinderblock houses, mobile homes, and propane tanks.

Minutes later they crossed over the Rio Pescado bridge and entered the outskirts of Zuni. Flat stone and adobe houses appeared on both sides of the highway, their dusty yards separated by rickety juniper fences and patches of green corn and yellow sunflowers. Speeding by, the landscape became an abstract painting—green and yellow splotches on a brown canvas.

Chickens, goats, and dogs wandered freely from yard to yard and down into the sandy ditch alongside the highway. As they came into the center of the pueblo he could smell bread baking in the beehive ovens and then the warm fragrant scent of mutton stew cooking in the roadside stands. The smells reminded him of camping in the mountains. Good smells. Good memories.

Antonio braked suddenly for a scruffy gray goat eating grass at the edge of the highway, oblivious to the traffic. "I don't know how to get to the mission church, do you?"

He didn't, so Antonio turned into the busy parking lot next

to the tribal office. Trucks and four-wheel drive vehicles jammed the parking lot, with a small group of Zunis gathered near the food booths along the road.

Finding a parking space proved impossible, Antonio double-parked in the fire lane next to a brown Mazda pickup with its tailgate down. Three Zuni men sat on the tailgate talking and passing around a water jug. All three wore straw hats, with leather work gloves stuck in the back pockets of their jeans. They laughed when Antonio drove up, then fell silent, staring at the two strangers.

"*Bueños dias*," Antonio said.

The Zuni closest to them nodded and then said something to his companions that made them all laugh again.

"Wait here, I'll be right back." He jumped out of the car.

Antonio frowned. "Thanks a lot."

Ignoring the tension, he climbed out of the car and walked under the ramada in front of the tribal office. He made sure to remove his sunglasses and drop them in his shirt pocket before entering the building, noticing the thick adobe walls and the murals inside, painted on the rough brown stucco.

He found the information window just inside the door, where a woman with long dark hair and glasses stood behind the counter writing in a ledger book. The woman ignored him.

"Excuse me, I'm looking for the mission church."

The woman looked at him indifferently. "There's nothing going on there right now."

"I'm not a tourist. I'm looking for an abandoned car the highway patrol reported this afternoon." He showed her his badge.

The woman's expression did not change. She pointed to the east. "Go back to the first street, turn right and follow it around. You'll come to the church."

"Thanks," he said, then turned slowly and walked back outside.

Antonio looked glad to see him. "Where to?"

He repeated the directions.

The three Zunis watched them pull away from the curb, making sure the Plymouth didn't get too close to their pickup.

Back on the main road, Antonio took the first right turn,

a narrow road squeezed between juniper fences and crumbling stone walls. The road curved around to the right, behind clusters of stone and adobe houses, their flat roofs and protruding vigas visible over the tops of the fences.

The pueblo seemed to close in on them gradually, then all at once, as they entered a dusty plaza surrounded by multi-level stone houses connected by stone walls and a network of ladders. The ancient mission church stood at the rear of the plaza, a massive adobe structure with a second-floor balcony and a bell tower overlooking an enclosed graveyard in front. The graveyard was set off from the rest of the plaza by a waist-high adobe wall.

Antonio parked by the wall, next to a blue Honda Accord with a Bernalillo County license plate and a University of New Mexico parking sticker. Wanda LeClair's car.

He eased himself out of the Plymouth and stretched his muscles. For the moment he decided to ignore the flurry of activity on the far side of the plaza, where a highway patrol car and a Jeep belonging to the Tribal Police were parked side by side, their occupants conferring with an old Zuni woman who stood with her arms wrapped around a young boy, pressing him tight against her apron.

A highway patrolman and two Tribal Police officers crowded the old woman, asking questions all at once. No wonder the kid was scared, he decided.

Feeling a dozen sets of eyes watching him from doorways and behind windows, he took a moment to look inside the Honda. There was an empty soda bottle on the floor and stacks of papers and manila file folders littered the back seat. A mess. He tried the Honda's doors, which were unlocked, and was about to climb inside when he heard Antonio behind him.

"Look at this."

Antonio stood leaning on an adobe wall, staring at the enclosed graveyard that encircled the mission church.

When he joined Antonio at the wall he understood immediately why Antonio had called him over. Neither of them spoke. Hidden by the wall, huge green tumbleweeds had overgrown the entire graveyard, threatening to choke the fragile wooden crosses that marked the graves. The tumbleweeds had been allowed to grow wild, and yet all the crosses were freshly painted and decorated with brightly colored flowers and intricate ornaments. What he saw took his breath away.

He stepped back, shocked by the contrast, the graves so carefully tended, the tumbleweed ignored.

Feeling even more like a foreigner, he turned his back on the graveyard and walked across the plaza, while the highway patrolman and the Tribal Police officers waited for him.

"I'm Detective Lopez from Santa Fe." He showed his badge. "We're looking for the woman who owns this car. What's the story?"

The highway patrolman deferred to the Tribal Police.

"Two men left it here this afternoon," one of the officers said, a stocky Zuni whose uniform consisted of a khaki shirt and jeans.

The other Zuni officer motioned to the old woman protecting the child. "Tola saw them leave the car. We think they wanted it to look like a tourist's car. Like the driver came here and got lost or something."

"We haven't found the woman yet, but we have a description of the vehicle the two men drove away in," the highway patrolman added, eager to contribute something to the conversation.

Fernando frowned. "No matter," he said, raising his voice so that everyone could hear. "We know where to find her."

Part Two: Wanda LeClair

13

Tossing and turning in the bed she had shared with her lover, Wanda LeClair reached out for Michael Soto, remembering his touch on her naked body, how he had made her feel alive after so many years of denying herself the pleasures of the flesh. She moaned, feeling his head between her legs, his tongue darting in and out until she cried out for him to stop, to come inside. Then his slow, gentle way of making love, never rushing but postponing as long as possible that final, desperate rush to orgasm when she would pull him deeper and beg him to come with her.

Half awake, she felt his absence in the bed. Now and forever the love of her life would only be a memory. The only man who had ever triggered in her such an intense physical response was dead. Murdered.

She was left wondering if she would be next.

She couldn't remember if she had dead-bolted and chained the door to her room at La Fonda. She worried the person who killed Michael might come after her next. The two of them had shared a business, and although she hadn't been involved in Michael's black market dealings, his killer had no way of knowing that.

She got out of bed and checked the door. When she saw the dead-bolt and chain in place, she climbed back in bed and tried to fall asleep. She took another sleeping pill, because the first one wasn't working.

Exhausted now, she had no more tears to shed. She just wanted to sleep, but her jumbled thoughts kept her awake. She couldn't stop thinking about Michael, about how he could be here one day and gone forever the next. It seemed unreal. She didn't even have a chance to say goodbye. Above all, the question she could not get out of her mind was this—how could she have ended up in this room at La Fonda, alone and grieving? How?

Before Michael entered her life, she had been a reasonably happy woman. She loved her job teaching Cultural Anthropology at UNM, the familiar routine of teaching, research, and committee work. She loved the campus, as beautiful as any she had seen. Everything in her life was familiar, safe, just the way she'd always imagined. She might have gone on this way forever, going from her apartment in Albuquerque to her office in the Anthropology Building to her research carrel at Zimmerman Library. Then she'd met Michael and all that seemed so lonely, so empty. She realized what had been missing from her safe, tidy life.

She'd worked so hard for so long, first at San Diego State and then at Berkeley for graduate study. As soon as she finished her PhD, she applied for and received a faculty appointment at the University of New Mexico.

At UNM she went to work with a vengeance, spending her first three years writing a book on the various methods employed by the Spanish to subjugate the Pueblo people.

She remembered the years fondly. She enjoyed visiting the pueblos, driving up to Taos to watch the Corn Dance or out to Zuni to hike around the ruins of Hawikuh. She spent more time at Jémez than at any of the others, but her favorite pueblo to visit was Acoma, the Sky City, halfway between Albuquerque and Zuni.

She loved to walk to the top of the mesa where the pueblo stood, 357 feet above the desert floor. Looking west from Acoma, she tried to imagine what it must have been like for the Acomites on that day in 1540 when they looked down in horror at the approaching army of Francisco Vasquez de Coronado. Perhaps they had been warned, having heard rumors of foreign invaders riding strange animals and carrying strange weapons. Only one year earlier the expedition of Friar Marcos de Nina and his Moorish slave Estevan had come up from Mexico as far north as Zuni, penetrating the boundaries of the Pueblo world. But no warning could have adequately prepared them for the four hundred years of death and destruction that followed the arrival of the Spanish.

Seen from afar, Coronado's soldiers might have appeared harmless enough, perhaps even comical. She liked to picture the scene—the Acomites watching from the top of their sandstone fortress, and the Spanish trudging across the desert with their horses and clumsy armor. The Spanish were not harmless, of course. By the time they pushed into the interior of North America they had already destroyed the great Aztec and Incan civilizations. But the Acomites would not have known about the fate of Montezuma or Manco Capac, and they would have believed that their gods would protect them so that they could continue living unaffected and harmoniously on their mesa as they had done for five hundred years. Here, too, they were wrong.

She felt an enormous sense of relief when her book was published and reviewed favorably in the appropriate scholarly journals. Because of the success of *When the Corn Mothers Wept: The Spanish Conquest of the Pueblo Indians*, she received tenure at the University of New Mexico and a research semester free to begin another book. For this second book she decided to narrow her focus. She chose a single Spanish colony, La Villa Real de San Francisco de la Santa Fe, built on the remains of Ogapoge Pueblo. Early Santa Fe provided her with a microcosm of Spanish control through the hated "encomendra" system. Under this system, Spanish settlers of the appropriate rank and gender were given huge tracts of land as well as trusteeship of all Native American people who happened to live on the land, which sometimes included entire pueblos. The Indians became slaves, forced to work for their masters on a rotating basis and to pay tributes of cloth and grain twice each year.

And what did the Pueblo people get in return? They received protection and so-called religious instruction. What a bargain. She could scarcely contain her sarcasm. Especially as she worked her way through the Spanish documents housed in the State Records Center, meticulously collecting evidence for her new study. Her research had been proceeding according to the schedule she had devised for herself. Then one afternoon she met Michael and her life changed forever. It was both an end and a beginning.

She'd been a fool for love, no doubt about that.

When they'd met last Spring at the opening of a new exhibit at the Indian Pueblo Cultural Center, she found herself powerfully attracted to this man who fascinated her with his outgoing personality and, of course, his looks. They shared the same lifelong interest in Native American Art—he sold it, she taught it. They spent the afternoon talking in the coffee shop at the Center and then continued over dinner across the street at the Range Café. He promised romance, excitement, all the intimacy she had denied herself through her years in graduate school and then her professorship at UNM

That first day they ended up in her apartment drinking wine and continuing their conversation. It was only a pretext, however. They both knew what they wanted. She made the first move, and before she knew it they were in her bed, naked. He was a slow, generous lover, allowing her to climb on top and move up and down until she finished.

Soon she came to believe Michael was the love of her life. When he walked into her apartment or office, it was like electricity crackled all around her, a physical sensation that eventually consumed her waking hours, not to mention her dreams. They talked, they made plans, and eventually she decided to resign her academic position at UNM in order to manage Sabado Indian Arts in Santa Fe and become Michael's...what? Lover and business partner, maybe even his wife eventually, although they never really spoke about that, never really had enough time together to have that conversation.

When she left her apartment in Albuquerque and moved in with him at La Fonda until his new house in Hyde Park Estates could be finished, she had no idea where their relationship was leading, not a clue. Michael did not like to talk about the future, preferring to postpone major decisions until the time was right, until the issue was at hand and could be postponed no longer.

The here and now was enough for him, he would say. Until now, ironically, when there was no more here and now.

What she discovered over the summer was that Sabado wasn't generating all that much income, not nearly enough to support his—and her—lifestyle. So where did the money come from? At first she denied what she suspected he was doing when he began attending peyote ceremonies and driving by himself, sometimes late at night, to meet various "clients" who procured for him tribal artifacts and ceremonial items, which Michael then sold to mysterious dealers or collectors from far-flung places like Washington DC, New York, even Paris.

Michael wouldn't show her the items he bought on the black market, keeping them in a locked closet until he had just the right buyer with just the right money.

They argued last week over the locked closet. She wanted him to swear he wasn't dealing stolen tribal goods to these buyers. He swore he wasn't, but she didn't really believe him. A week later he was dead, murdered at one of the peyote ceremonies. And where was she now, having lost her job at UNM, her apartment, and all the intimacy and fine things Michael Soto had promised?

She felt trapped. Surely the police detective who brought her news about Michael's murder would suspect her involvement in Michael's illegal business. How would she explain? How could she convince him that she had fallen in love with Michael and had no idea that he was involved in the black market Indian trade. Why would he believe her?

The fact that Michael had left Sabado Indian Arts to her in his will made her situation worse, because now she would be the sole proprietor of the gallery and therefore legally responsible. She found herself in legal jeopardy with no clear way out.

Desperate, she decided to do the only thing she could think of to make amends and clear her record. She found the key to Michael's locked closet, packed all the artifacts in bubble-wrap, and boxed them in heavy cardboard containers.

Two of the items had tags marked "Hawikuh," the ancient Zuni ruin, but the rest were unmarked. She forced herself not to individually examine the precious pottery, gourds, and carvings that she packed, telling herself that she would not be held responsible for them if she did not know what they were. How could she?

The only thing she could think to do was to get rid of the artifacts quickly, before the police detective returned. And he would return, she was sure of that. Then it occurred to her—John Reno and his Whitewater Zuni Traders. She knew from what Michael had told her that Reno dealt in the illegal Indian trade. Reno would take the objects back and she would be free of responsibility.

Yes, Whitewater was the solution. She could stop at Zuni along the way and visit an old friend who had helped her back when she was doing ethnographic research at Zuni. He might even help her return some of the items. The rest she would take to Whitewater Zuni Traders and give to John Reno, just give him everything and be done with it.

While she imagined the scene, replaying it over and over in her mind, she began to feel drowsy until her memory began to fog. Through the fog she found herself freefalling through the vast darkness of space. Far below her she saw the faint lights of candles and campfires of an ancient city, peopled by shrouded figures moving among the shadows from the Plaza to the Santa Fe River.

14

Dreaming, she arose from her bed and went out into the night. She moved as though floating on air, her long white robe shimmering in the moonlight. The quarter moon hung low in the sky, suspended above the triangular peaks of the mountains and the newly built city nestled in the valley below. La Villa Real de la Santa Fe de San Francisco de Asis, city of mud houses and mud streets surrounded by a seven-foot mud wall. Seen from afar, the city pulsed with the yellow glow of candles and open fires scattered among the adobes and along the banks of the Santa Fe River.

The lone sentry did not notice her as she passed through an opening in the wall, hovering a few inches off the ground, floating on a current of air that carried her down toward the plaza. Past the governor's fields and corrals, where the horses, sensing her presence, stirred restlessly. Down to the Casas Reales, the government buildings, where the governor lived with his store of supplies, which he sold to the Spanish soldiers and settlers. When she rounded the corner, she saw two helmeted sentries, armed with lances, guarding the entrance to the Casas Reales. The sentries tended a raging bonfire that illuminated the front facade, including the squat wooden towers constructed at both ends of the building.

Suddenly something on the plaza caught her attention. She turned her back on the bonfire and entered the dark plaza, an empty dirt lot overgrown with weeds. She saw a wooden cross about her height held together with twine and decorated with dead wilted flowers. And something else, over on the far side of the plaza near the garrison, the building that served as a barracks for all the unmarried Spanish soldiers except the few who belonged to the governor's special guard and who lived in the Casas Reales. Laughter and rowdy voices greeted her as she approached the garrison, a squat adobe building with heavy wooden doors, defended by two small cannons. The black, cast-iron cannons crouched like lions on either side of the door, untended at this hour.

The sight sent her reeling away from the garrison and up the street, where the lights of the "parroquia" beckoned her. From its position on a small hill overlooking the plaza, the church cast a faint yellow glow on the surrounding trees. The light poured out of the open doors and windows, illuminating the bell tower as she approached from below. Voices called her inside. Soft, distant voices, chanting prayers or singing, she couldn't tell which. Then the smell of incense and candle wax, smoke from a hundred candles flickering on the altar, reflecting off the brass and pewter candle holders.

She paused in the doorway, startled to find so many forlorn figures huddled on the crude wooden benches. Then, in a single second, a flicker of light, she realized that all of them were women. Spanish women, old and young, some wearing black shawls and some holding beads and prayer books.

The sounds blended together, merging into a sweet music that lured her down to the protective wall along the river, then beyond, outside the walled city of the Spanish. The music drew her across a log bridge into the Barrio de Analco. Music and the sound of human voices beckoned her, whispering for her to come, come deeper into the barrio.

She saw the small mud houses, packed tightly together, sprawling from the river as far as the Chapel of San Miguel, which the Spanish had built especially for their slaves across the river and outside the walls of their city.

The slaves lived in makeshift dwellings, lean-tos assembled from whatever scrap wood and pine boughs they could find along the river and in the hills to the east. Others slept out in the open, huddled around fires in the fields where they worked. When their period of servitude expired, they would be replaced by a fresh herd of slaves from the nearby pueblos.

No longer afraid, she entered the maze of mud huts, finding her way along a narrow street that connected to a central plaza area, where wood coals in the bee-hive ovens still smoldered from the day's baking. The ovens radiated the smell of fresh bread, along with the stronger scent of burning piñon. She went among the Indian women, some of them even shorter than her, their bodies wrapped in blankets and their dark faces partly hidden by shawls. Under the thatched roof of one lean-to three women were grinding corn at separate metate stones, while an old man squatted on the packed earth and played a flute to keep time, the rhythm of the metate. As she watched she began to feel the rhythm, like a pulse deep inside her that grew louder until it enveloped her entire body in waves of sound.

When the flute music stopped, she moved off toward the larger houses near the Chapel of San Miguel, some of them with strands of dried corn and chile hanging from the adobe walls. Up ahead a tall, shrouded figure squeezed between two mud walls and walked quickly through the maze of houses and open fires. Her silk scarf, her farthingale, and her fine leather sandals marked her as a Spanish woman from across the river. But why would a Spanish woman of obvious means come to the Barrio de Analco as this hour of the night?

She followed the fleeting woman to the milpas, the Indian fields at the edge of the barrio, where a round Navajo-style hogan stood beside an open pit fire. The fire looked untended, but as they approached she saw the blanket over the door of the hogan stir and an old woman step out to greet them, as though she had somehow known they were coming. Hobbling with the aid of a walking stick, the old woman motioned for the Spanish woman to sit on a wooden bench by the fire, then turned sharply and pointed her stick directly at her. Instantly the stick changed into a huge snake with red eyes and white fangs that twisted in the air hissing.

When she sank back in fear, the old woman smiled, toothless and wrinkled. Then the hideous old woman slowly lowered the serpent until it touched the ground, changing back into a walking stick. Even then the hissing continued. Wanda watched the old woman hobble over to the fire and turn her attention to the Spanish woman.

"Beatriz, my husband continues to be unfaithful," the Spanish woman said. "I need a stronger potion than the one you gave me before."

She recognized the name. The old woman was Beatriz de los Angeles, a *bruja* famous for the love and fertility potions she prescribed for the women who enlisted her services. Beatriz and her daughter Juana both possessed the *mal ojo* or evil eye that made their victims, usually men, sicken and eventually die.

Men feared the avenging Beatriz, because at night she would transport herself through the air searching for the frequent paramours of the young and beautiful Juana. On her nocturnal flights Beatriz punished the men who succumbed to her temptress daughter. The powers of Beatriz could wilt even the strongest man.

The old woman eased herself down on the bench next to the Spanish woman. Her eyes reflected the red glow of the coals still smoking in the fire pit. "First you must tell me this. Do you want your husband to live or to die?"

"To live, of course," the Spanish woman said, after a slight pause. She removed her scarf, revealing a thin, emaciated face. The face of a bird.

"Then you must give him this powdered calabaza and chan." Beatriz took a small cloth bag from under her robe. "This time don't put it in his food. Make a paste with water and rub it between your legs and on his loins during sexual relations. If that doesn't work, then collect his urine, or the urine of his mistress, and rub it on your body. Then, surely, love will return."

The Spanish woman accepted the small bag and held it to her nose, sniffing.

"Do you understand?"

The Spanish woman nodded.

"If you decide you want your husband to die, come back and I will give you a mixture of garbancillo for him and his mistress."

"Thank you." The Spanish woman gave Beatriz a small coin

and then, wrapping her scarf tightly around her face, hurried off in the direction of the river.

After the woman had gone, Beatriz looked at Wanda and laughed.

She watched the old woman hobble back to the hogan and disappear inside. Suddenly feeling alone and exposed, she turned to look for the Spanish woman, already out of sight. Coyotes and witches howled behind her as she began to walk quickly toward the comforting lights of the barrio. Too afraid to look back, she heard the serpent's hissing sound and felt the sting of sharp fangs nipping at her ankles. She imagined coiled serpents behind every clump of sage. Witches in every shadow.

Suddenly the wind picked up and the moon went behind a bank of clouds, plunging the terrain in front of her into total darkness. Dust swirled around her legs, creating a vortex that lifted her high into the air, then dropped her gently on a hillside near the Chapel of San Miguel. Boiling clouds of white fog appeared at the top of the hill, rolling down the slope like giant boulders about to crush her.

While she watched fearfully, the tumbling clouds parted and the shape of an ox-cart began to materialize, black against the white fog. The cart moved slowly down the hill and out of the fog, its heavy wooden wheels creaking loudly as they traversed the rough terrain, over rocks and dead wood that snapped like bones. She gasped when she saw the black, shrouded figure pulling the cart. Not a person, not one of the living, but a skeleton wrapped in a long black shroud that billowed in the wind, revealing the bony arms and legs underneath. She looked into the green, mummified face partly covered with patches of dried skin and stringy hair. Only the swollen red eyes looked alive, burning like fires in the dark.

"Doña Sebastiana," she called out, addressing death by its familiar name.

Pausing, Doña Sebastiana turned to look at her, beginning to raise the bow and arrow that she always carried.

Only then did she notice the second figure, a man sitting in the rear of the death cart. His body slumped forward, his head dangled into his lap. Wanda stepped closer to get a better view, hesitating when she glimpsed the man's forehead—a massive bleeding wound. Blood flowed freely down his face, pouring onto his shirt and pants. Rivers of gushing blood that filled the bottom of the death cart and spilled out onto the ground.

As if in slow motion, the man began to raise his head. Trying to look at her. Trying to speak.

Her whole body began to shake. She recognized him, just as surely as he recognized her.

Suddenly his head snapped back, his neck twisting at a sharp angle, and she found herself looking directly into the swollen, discolored face of Michael Soto.

Still, she didn't scream until she saw, out of the corner of her eye, Doña Sebastiana cock her bow and arrow and take aim directly at her.

15

Following her plan, she drove west on I-40 across vast stretches of flat desert, the monotony of the landscape broken by distant mesas, pink and gray against the bright morning sky. Instead of going to Gallup and then dropping down to Zuni, she turned off the interstate at Grants, following Highway 53 as it entered the black lava hills of the Malpais, the ridges of gnarled, porous rock looking like the spines of ancient dinosaurs. Once out of the Malpais, the highway swung west and followed the route of the ancient Acoma-Zuni Trail across the Continental Divide.

She drove past El Morro and Inscription Rock, the prow-like mesa that served as the most prominent landmark along the trail. She didn't bother to stop at the visitor center, not wanting to waste precious time.

Soon she drove through the small Mormon town of Ramah, with the rounded foothills of the Zuni Mountains to the north, covered with piñon and juniper and occasionally a tall ponderosa pine.

Whenever she came to Zuni, she realized how fortunate the Zuni were to be so isolated from the large urban centers of the Southwest. Their isolation had allowed them to preserve their distinct and highly ceremonial culture, unaffected by the tourists that flocked to most of the other pueblos in New Mexico. The Zuni opened their pueblo to the public on certain ceremonial occasions, most notably for the great Shalako dances during the winter solstice, but otherwise visitors were not encouraged and not terribly well received

Not tourists, but ethnographers like herself had been the

problem at Zuni. Ironically, because of its isolation, Zuni became all the more attractive to academics wanting to do fieldwork in a culture unexposed to European ways. Ethnographers like Frank Cushing, Edward Sapir, Franz Boas, and Ruth Bunzel.

The long drive gave her time to reflect on these and other matters. Clearly John Reno or someone working with him had uncovered materials from Hawikuh, the original pueblo visited by the Spanish in the sixteenth century. Hawikuh had been excavated repeatedly, most thoroughly by the archaeologist Frederick Hodge from 1917 to 1923. But there were always more artifacts to be discovered by looters and grave robbers, people willing to destroy the fragile ruins to get at the treasures buried underneath the walls.

She decided to make a stop in Zuni before going on to Whitewater. Her friend Johnny Peywa, a former governor of Zuni who had come to UNM on several occasions to lecture in her Southwestern Anthropology class, would know of any recent digging at Zuni, legal or otherwise.

Entering Zuni was not like entering any of the other pueblos. Zuni sprawled along both sides of the highway, the flat houses constructed of adobe and brown rock, separated by patchwork fields and stick corrals, with clusters of beehive ovens and abandoned cars. Only in the heart of the old pueblo did multi-story dwellings still exist, three and four levels of rooms built on top of one another with wooden rafters and ladder-poles jutting into the sky.

She thought she remembered how to get to Peywa's house.

Just before the long parking lot that extended from the post office to the tribal offices next door, she turned left and followed the narrow blacktop into a maze of cedar fences and adobe walls. Looking for the right driveway, she slowed to a crawl and opened her window. Even so, she would have missed it if she hadn't seen the bundle of golden eagle feathers, brown with white speckles, tied to a thin cedar pole. The feathers sparked her memory, and suddenly she recognized the fence and the long unpaved driveway.

Halfway down the driveway, she saw Pewya's wife, wearing a white cotton dress, tying clusters of shucked corn and then hanging them to dry on wires stretched between cedar poles. The yellow corn looked like clusters of ripe bananas.

She waved at her and the old woman waved back tentatively, not recognizing Wanda.

Nearing the house, she left the driveway and drove across the hard-packed earth, pulling up behind an old Ford Bronco, its black fenders dented and rusted from years of hard use. She smiled when she saw Peywa sitting in a rocking chair under a tin ramada that extended out from the front of his adobe house. Eyes closed, the old man appeared to be asleep, a can of Pepsi stuck between his legs. But when she opened her car door, he raised his head, studying the dusty little car that looked so out of place parked in his front yard. Then he struggled to his feet and, still holding his can of Pepsi, came out to meet her.

"*Keshshé,*" he said, his brown, wrinkled face breaking into a smile. "Hello."

"*Keshshé.*" She noticed how feeble he looked. She thought he had lost some weight. He wore a khaki shirt and baggy jeans held up by red suspenders.

"You look well."

She shielded her eyes from the sun. "So do you."

"Not so good. *Halow samu*. Too many bad dreams."

She laughed, feeling pleasantly comfortable with Peywa, as she always did. He treated her like a daughter, and she enjoyed it.

"What brings you to Zuni?"

Suddenly she lost her composure. All the stress of the last few days seemed to overwhelm her all at once. She felt limp, with no more energy to keep up the good fight. She burst into tears.

Peywa said nothing. He put his arm around her shoulders and said, "Come. Sit with me."

16

They sat in adjoining rocking chairs on the porch. She was quieter now, having told Peywa everything about her bad decision to get involved with Michael and his illegal dealings in stolen tribal artifacts. She'd apologized profusely, asking his forgiveness and promising to return the stolen property that was now in her possession. Peywa said he would help her return the items, if they were Zuni. When she showed him the contents of the boxes she'd packed at Sabado, he spotted the two items marked "Hawikuh," a small pot with a pouring spout and a gourd.

"These we can return them to Hawikuh. Nobody has to know they were missing."

She gave him a hug. "Thank you."

Peywa brought her a cold Pepsi from inside the house. The two sat in silence, sipping their cold drinks and watching Peywa's wife as she continued to work under the hot sun, tying one cluster of corn after another and then hanging them neatly on the wire. The old woman glanced occasionally in their direction but made no effort to join them. Beyond her a row of yellow sunflowers swayed in the gentle breeze.

"So what else has been going on at Zuni?"

"Last week we had the Zuni Fair. Lotta people came for that. For the rodeo and the dances."

"That's right, I'd forgotten about the fair. I came up last year... or was it the year before? I especially liked the goat-tying contest."

Peywa chuckled. "That's not as easy as it looks—goat-tying."

She laughed. "It doesn't look easy to me."

Peywa closed his eyes and rocked quietly for a time. Finally he said, "Yeah, I heard about the digging. Down on the road to

Ojo Caliente. Someone's been digging at night."

"How far from Ojo Caliente? Near Hawikuh?"

Peywa nodded. "Between Hawikuh and the river."

"How long ago was the digging? Recently?"

"No, maybe late spring, early summer. Like that."

"Maybe that's where we should return the stolen artifacts. Maybe that's where they came from."

Peywa thought about this for a moment. He sighed. "Okay, we can do that, give them back to where they belong."

Peywa eased himself out of the rocking chair and tossed the empty Pepsi cans into a garbage can beside the house. "Okay."

Then, after putting his hands on his hips and delicately stretching his back muscles, he went to tell his wife about the plan to drive to Ojo Caliente.

She took the opportunity to visit the outhouse. During her visits she'd grown accustomed to the gray weathered structure, though she didn't exactly relish the thought of sitting on the rough wooden seats.

By the time she hitched up her jeans and walked back to the house, Peywa was standing beside her Honda, shaking his head at the small foreign automobile.

"Let's take mine." He motioned toward his Bronco. "This one's no good for where we're going."

She didn't argue, climbing into the Bronco and slamming the clunky door.

Peywa skillfully negotiated the ruts of the driveway, waving to his wife on the way out.

Once they hit the blacktop, she began to relax, enjoying the ride and the sights along the way, pleased to see all the mid-day activity in front of the tribal office—the colorful pickups and campers, the pottery and jewelry stands, the Zuni farmers selling squash and melon from the back of their flat-bed trucks. Then out into the desert, turning left on State Road 32, the road to Ojo Caliente and the sacred Zuni salt lake.

How beautiful the landscape looked. She wanted to mention it to Peywa, but of course he already knew. What was the Zuni word for beauty? *Tso'ya,* she thought. Flat-topped mesas receding into the distance, changing color with the slant of the sun, from gray-blue to yellow-brown to late afternoon shades of red and purple. Thunder Mountain on the left, and ahead of them an expanse of blue sagebrush and fields of yellow sunflowers, sprinkled with patches of Indian paintbrush and bee balm.

She didn't have sufficient words to express how much she loved New Mexico.

They stopped once to let a young sheepherder and his border collie drive a herd of hot, dirty sheep across the gravel road.

She left everything to Peywa, who hummed happily as he steered the Bronco. When he downshifted, studying the terrain on the right side of the road, Wanda realized they'd come to the end of their journey.

Peywa slowed the Bronco to a crawl, pointing to a gentle rise in the sagebrush. "This way, I think."

"I don't know." She had been to Hawikuh only once, many years before, when she'd first started working at UNM

Eventually Peywa found what he was looking for: a narrow service road that climbed the sandy bank on the right side of the road and then angled off, disappearing into the sagebrush.

"Hold on." He turned sharply into the ditch and then gunned the big motor.

She grabbed the overhead handle as they bounced over the embankment and landed heavily in a cloud of dust. The Bronco sputtered and swerved to the left, swiping a bank of chamisa, before Peywa managed to get control, wrestling the steering wheel sharply to the right. Still humming, he seemed unaffected by the rough ride as he began to pick up speed, oblivious to the thick red dust that nearly blinded her.

She breathed a sigh of relief when they finally stopped. She climbed out and carefully cradled the precious artifacts they were returning in her arms. Peywa paused for a moment and then, without saying a word, began walking up a small incline, following a well-worn trail packed hard by the small hooves of countless sheep. The old man's spryness amazed her. Though she struggled to keep up, she fell further and further behind on the trail.

Peywa waited for her at the top, hands in the pockets of his baggy jeans. When she came over the rise, she felt the hot dry wind blowing out of the southwest and smelled the scent of the sagrebrush. Below her lay the golden-brown ruins of Hawikuh, a maze of chest-high stone walls partially drifted over by sand.

Like a giant honeycomb, built in layers of stone and mud mortar, the rooms varied in size and shape, some square, some rectangular, and some round. Windows and doors connected many of the rooms, adding to the labyrinth effect. She noticed the remains of the wooden rafters that five hundred years earlier had supported the upper levels of the pueblo. The sight was as impressive as she remembered.

Something moved halfway down the hill. From the corner of her eye she caught a glimpse of a large black object moving parallel to the river.

Seeing her jump, Peywa laughed and pointed to what turned out to be a horse feeding on the short grass near the riverbank.

Wild horses. There were three of them, moving slowly to the north, away from the scent of the humans who had interrupted their grazing.

Embarrassed by her giddiness, she made a face, mocking herself.

"The looters who dig here, they don't do it during the day, do they?"

"Only at night. Come, let me show you."

She followed him down the hill to a long narrow mound of dirt. Shovels and pickaxes had dug deep and then churned up good part of the mound, revealing a tangled trove of human bones—some of them smashed by the heavy metal instruments. Seeing the exposed bones filled her with hatred for whoever had done this. Can there be a more serious violation of human sanctity than destroying the bones of someone's ancestors? She didn't think so.

Peywa stood back from the hideous sight, shaking his head. "You see what they do? Looking for what?"

She made a futile gesture with her hands.

"They come from over in Arizona." Peywa pointed to the west. "Sometimes they circle down from Gallup. Take Highway sixty-one back across the New Mexico state line and then cut across the desert on the service roads. No one lives around here to catch them."

She looked to the west, the direction from which Coronado had come. Out of the west, the direction of the setting sun.

"Hapiya, a sheepherder, found the digging last month. By accident."

Peywa continued on toward the river, coming first to a shallow arroyo, no more than five feet deep, where he pointed to the collapsed banks and the mounds of loose sand piled at the bottom. Between the mounds of sand dozens of small black-on-white potsherds had been tossed together, discarded by the thieves looking for large ceramic fragments or entire pots, which could be sold to private collectors for outrageous prices.

Trying to keep up with Peywa, she cut through a prickly patch of sagebrush that caught at her jeans. She plodded awkwardly across the soft sand that made walking difficult.

Peywa pointed out more digging as he walked along, seemingly unaffected by the soft, slippery terrain. Apparently, the thieves had been looking for outlying houses or kivas separated from the main pueblo and possibly not as carefully excavated, if excavated at all. The digging sites were all shallow, as if the thieves had quickly given up and moved on to other locations.

"Up there." Peywa pointed to a flat-topped rise overlooking the river. The river cut a wide swath through the desert landscape, but only a brown trickle of water flowed down the center of the rocky riverbed, surrounded by salt brush and willows and a few scraggly cottonwoods already beginning to lose their leaves.

Halfway up the rise she spotted the ruin. Small, two or three rooms, the crumbling walls mostly buried in the white sand.

But as she came closer, she noticed the piles of sandy earth and something else—a hole in the floor of one of the rooms. The thieves had punched through to a sealed underground room, the dream of all the people who hunted illegally for pots and other Indian artifacts. A sealed room, untouched by human hands for sometimes hundreds of years. When discovered, usually by archaeologists on official digs, these rooms might contain valuable pots and baskets, sometimes ceremonial items and precious stones. Even human bones had been found.

Peywa pointed to one of the niches in the wall. "Dig it out

and bury them deep. The grave robbers won't be back. They've already looted the room."

So the two of them dug out the niche, which was cut deep into the stone wall. They unwrapped the tribal objects, placed them gently in the niche, and then packed sand and loose rock around their burial. To make it look undisturbed they sprinkled sand and dirt and dried plants around the opening.

Peywa mumbled something under his breath, a prayer of some sort. A benediction.

17

Halfway to Whitewater she came to a sudden realization. She had no idea what to say to John Reno. Should she simply give him the boxes in her trunk and then leave? Should she ask him to return the objects to where they belonged? Should she tell him to stop looting and selling stolen tribal objects on the black marker? Should she threaten to call the police and tell them everything? She wasn't sure, never having met Reno and not knowing what to expect.

What worried her now, at this late date, was the fear that he had been involved in Michael's murder. Was Reno a murderer?

Driving north on Highway 32, she tried to devise a strategy. But no matter how she played out the scene in her mind she couldn't imagine Reno agreeing to end his black market trade. No, it would be safer to drop off the boxes of artifacts and get out fast. Once she returned to Santa Fe she could call detective Lopez and tell him about Michael and Reno and how she'd gotten herself involved in all this mess. Hopefully the detective would understand her situation and cut her some slack for being a whistleblower, for trying to do the right thing.

North of Zuni the sagebrush flats gave way to more rugged terrain, where rock formations and box canyons rose up out of an ocean of rolling hills dotted with piñon and juniper. Though she'd driven this road before, she couldn't remember much about the town of Whitewater. The town existed only on paper. In reality it wasn't a town so much as a few distant houses set back from the highway, as though the people who built them desired to resist any connection to one another.

How different from Zuni, which she'd left only minutes before, where the sense of connection defined every aspect of life. But she had no time to compare cultures now, no time to do anything but step on the brake pedal and slow down as she approached the Whitewater 7-Eleven, as nondescript as every other 7-Eleven. Gas pumps in front, white styrofoam coolers and cases of soft drinks piled on the sidewalk and stacked inside the front window.

She turned right, coming to a stop at the edge of the parking lot. Then she spotted Whitewater Zuni Traders, less than a hundred yards up the highway on the left side of the road. No wonder she hadn't noticed it before, because it sat back from the highway on a small hill. From where she parked, she had a clear view of the building, gray stone with a tin roof and black iron grates on the windows. To the north, across a dusty yard of weeds and patches of cheat grass, stood a mobile home shimmering white in the afternoon sun.

Another stone structure, about thirty yards behind the trading post, seemed to emerge out of the side of a bluff, a putty-colored van parked alongside. Some kind of dug-out, she guessed, noticing how a distant ridge extended in a semicircle around the buildings, offering protection from the wind and whatever else might come across the uninhabited expanse of desert to the west. The Whitewater Zuni Traders sign, bright white letters painted on natural pine, marked the long driveway that led to a small gravel parking lot, empty now except for a silver Jeep Cherokee.

Before meeting Reno, she decided to buy a cold drink at the 7-Eleven. A caffeinated drink. She needed a jump-start, a burst of quick energy. Making sure to take her keys, she walked across the parking lot, which reeked of spilled gasoline and oil-burning cars, and entered the cluttered convenience store. The teenager behind the counter gave her a passing nod and returned to his paperback. She took a bottle of Coke out of the cooler and brought it to the front counter.

"Can I help you?" he asked, putting the book on a shelf behind the counter after carefully marking his page.

"Just this," she said.

He took her five dollar bill and gave her back some change.

"Thanks." He reached for his paperback.

"Do you know John Reno, the owner of the trading post?" she asked.

The kid shrugged. "Not really. I mean he comes in for gas and stuff, but I don't really know him. He's not around much. I think he travels a lot, stuff like that. I don't know."

"What does he sell over there? Anything I might be interested in?"

"I don't know," he said. "Indian stuff, I guess. Why, are you selling something?"

She smiled. "No, just curious."

She stepped outside and twisted off the plastic top on her Coke. She took a drink, and then walked back to her car to finish the bottle. The dose of sugar and caffeine energized her. Feeling more energetic, she drove up the highway and turned into the driveway of the trading post, her tires spinning in the loose gravel. The little Honda bounced up the driveway and into the parking lot. She pulled in beside the Jeep Cherokee.

Up close the gray stone building looked older, probably dating from the early 1900s. Older and much darker. The iron bars on the windows gave the trading post a somber, prison-like appearance. Not the kind of place that would attract tourists driving down to Zuni or up to the Indian markets in Gallup. But that came as no surprise. She knew Reno sold to a more exclusive clientele, including gallery owners like Michael and wealthy collectors.

So mustering her courage, she climbed out of her car and walked briskly up the flagstone sidewalk to the trading post. Opening the front door, she entered a dark cavernous room that smelled vaguely of mold and old leather. As her eyes adjusted to the darkness, she noticed a tall Zuni woman in a red blanket dress cleaning a glass display case with a bottle of Windex and a roll of paper towels.

Tall and athletic, the woman turned to stare at her, her shoulder-length black hair framing the dark eyes and long handsome face. Everything about the woman made her uneasy—the way she positioned herself in front of the display case, as though blocking her path. The way she held her body rigid, without any expression on her face, without the slightest trace of interest in the customer standing before her.

She felt an undercurrent of hostility. Bad vibes. Buy why? "Excuse me, I'm looking for John Reno. Is he available?"

The woman continued to stare with her dark eyes. Finally she nodded. "*Keshshé,*" she said, her voice strangely muffled.

She decided the woman was not so much unfriendly as awkward. Very likely she spoke only limited English, a characteristic common among Zunis of her generation. And anyway, the Zunis had a well-deserved reputation for being inhospitable to outsiders. Who could blame them?

"*Keshshé,*" she said.

The woman turned to go, then paused. "*Tosh kwayi*?"

"No, I'll wait here."

The woman nodded, again with great formality, then disappeared behind the counter and through an archway leading to an interior room.

Glad for the chance to look around, she went over to the glass display case and found a collection of what looked to be very old and rare pots. Most of the pieces were either chipped or cracked, but two remained magnificently intact. She thought she recognized the first as a Mimbres bowl, gray with delicate black lines painted around the rim and in the bottom of the bowl. She felt more certain about the second, a ceramic jar much larger than the bowl, prominently displayed on a white cloth in the center of the case. The rosy color of the jar, shaped like an urn with a two-inch opening in the top, suggested it was Anasazi of the type known as St. John's Polychrome.

Not an expert on ceramics, she couldn't date the pots with any degree of precision, but she guessed they must be five or six hundred years old. They were exquisitely beautiful...and incredibly valuable. So what were they doing in an unlocked display case?

The strangeness of the place became more apparent as she looked around. For one thing, she saw no price tags. Not on the pots, not on the Navajo rugs stacked in the corner, and not on the Indian jewelry in the back of the display case.

She admired the sand-cast silver bracelets and the selection of Zuni in-lay jewelry. Magnificent workmanship, but poor lighting made the room and everything in it seem a bit dreary. The only artificial light came from two bare bulbs that hung from the ceiling above the counter. Hardly enough light to read price tags, had there been any.

Footsteps in the back room ended her inspection, reminding her that she was not alone. Strengthening her resolve, she turned to meet Reno.

"What can I do for you?" he asked, bursting through the archway, his boot heels clicking on the rough-cut pine floor.

A barrel-chested man with legs so thin they looked like toothpicks, Reno stood well over six feet tall, with thinning red hair that made his pale skin look even paler and a drooping handlebar mustache twisted at the corners. He wore skin-tight jeans and a black pearl-buttoned shirt.

Everything about the man screamed "cowboy," including his enormous silver belt buckle with the letters J R encircled by a rope design.

"Hello," she said, smiling with as much bravado as she could muster. She stuck out her hand. "I'm Wanda LeClair, the manager of Michael Soto's gallery in Santa Fe."

After an awkward pause, Reno reached across the counter and shook her hand limply. "Pleased to meet you."

"Interesting place you have here," she said, glancing around the room. She noticed the Zuni woman watching from the shadows just inside the archway.

"We get by," Reno drawled.

As though on cue, the woman emerged from the shadows and returned to her work cleaning the glass case.

As Reno studied her, she wished she hadn't worn jeans and a silk blouse. She should have dressed more professionally.

"You know about Michael? That he was murdered?"

Reno nodded.

"That's why I'm here. I mean..." She struggled to explain.

Reno twisted the ends of his handlebar mustache. "What do you want?"

Suddenly it occurred to her as she stared at the red splotches on Reno's ugly white hands that he had been the one who killed Michael. It seemed so obvious now, looking at Reno's demeanor.

She felt her heart beating rapidly. She should have guessed earlier, when she was trying to come up with a plan. She had been careless.

"Let me tell you something about Soto," Reno said. "He had some big ideas—he thought he knew more than he did. These West Coast types, they think they can come out here and steal us blind, thinking we're a bunch of hicks. Well, Soto wasn't as slick as he thought he was. He double-crossed his friends, and he paid the price. You understand? The man was a thief."

How ironic, she thought, for Reno to stand there and accuse Michael of being a thief.

"Whoever killed him did us all a favor. That's what I think."

"Look, I know what you and Michael were doing," she blurted out. "About the illegal sales. The tribal objects."

Reno stared at her with a pained expression on his face.

"Michael left the gallery to me in his will, you see, but I want nothing to do with the black market. I found a closet where Michael kept the merchandise he bought illegally, but I don't want the stuff. So I brought it here...to give to you. You were his Zuni supplier, so I want to give it back, all of it. It's in the trunk of my car. I want you to take it back, please."

Reno listened without any noticeable reaction.

Just then, a red Ford pickup drove up outside.

Through the front windows she saw two men in dirty white T-shirts and jeans jump out of the pickup and unhook the tailgate. Coming toward the front door, one of them carried a wooden crate and the other a large canvas duffel bag.

Reno stepped out from behind the counter and hurried to the door. "Take it back to the shed," he instructed the men, opening the door only a crack. The two men did as they were told.

She pretended not to notice them as they carried their spoils around behind the trading post.

"Show me what you have," Reno said, finally.

She followed him outside to her Honda. While he stood back to observe, she popped the trunk and opened both cardboard boxes.

"There, take a look. That's everything I could find at Sabado, everything Michael had locked in his closet. I was hoping you could return the items to their rightful owners. Can you do that?"

Reno smiled. He leaned his tall frame over the trunk and carefully began unwrapping the objects in the boxes. Not saying a word, he took each and every parcel out of the two boxes, unwrapped it, and set it down on the carpet inside the trunk.

Finished, he rewrapped each one and placed it securely in the appropriate box. The entire procedure took several tense minutes, neither of them speaking.

He straightened up and stared at her. "And you want me to give these pieces to who?"

"Well, back to where they came from," she said, feeling more unsure of herself now, realizing how impractical and ridiculous her request must seem to a thief and murderer like Reno.

He laughed at her. "You want to tell me how I'm supposed to know where they came from?"

"Where you got them. Didn't most of the pieces come from you?"

He stared at her for several seconds before responding. "And if I do take the boxes, you're not going to tell the law what I'm doing? Is that right?"

"Yes...I won't say a word...if you stop selling tribal objects. I'll drive back to Santa Fe and pretend this exchange never happened. All I I want is for you to stop doing this. It's illegal. It's stealing tribal heritage. If you don't stop I'll be forced to go to the authorities. Surely you understand that any violation of the Antiquities Preservation Act carries a stiff penalty."

"Just who do you think you're talking to, lady?" Reno asked, his face turning red. "You think you can come in here and try to tell me what to do—"

"You did kill Michael, didn't you?" she said, interrupting him.

"Listen, you fucking bitch, Soto was cheating me. He cut into my business and underpaid me for the material I provided. Then he tried to sell me a fake carving for one of my clients. He got exactly what he deserved. Fuck Soto!"

"So you did kill him?"

The question hung in the air as Reno suddenly broke into an unexpected smile, white teeth emerging from under his long red mustache.

He burst out laughing.

Before she had time to react, she felt the strong arm of the Zuni woman grab her around the neck. The thick, muscular arm pulled her backwards, choking the air out of her windpipe and plunging her into darkness.

18

She lay bound and gagged on the hard floor struggling to free her hands and feet. Taped behind her back, her hands had lost more circulation than her feet. Every so often she clawed at the packed earth, trying to restore feeling in her fingers. The pain eased a little when she turned on her side, but within a few minutes her shoulder began to ache and the numbness returned, always worse than before. The more she fought, the more the tape dug into her raw, bleeding wrists.

Making matters worse, she couldn't see because of the hood over her head. While the Zuni woman held her, one of Reno's friends had come up from behind and stuffed a gag in her mouth and a white cotton hood over her head. The gag choked her at first, but she'd gotten used to that. Now the hood bothered her more, a drawstring at the bottom cutting into the soft tissue of her neck. Through the cloth she saw only a distant blur of objects. Nothing more.

Her initial panic had passed quickly. Now she only wanted to get comfortable. If she could get comfortable, maybe she could think of a plan. Find a way to cut through the tape by rubbing it against a rock or the sharp corner of a cabinet or doorway. There had to be a way out. People did escape from these predicaments, she reasoned with herself. The important thing was to be positive, no matter what. Don't let yourself fall into despair. No negativity, that was the key to getting out of this.

Thinking about escape made her feel ridiculous, as though she'd landed in some cheap Hollywood movie. Here she was, the heroine, bound and gagged and locked away in some storage shed in the middle of nowhere.

Waiting for the hero to appear, waiting for the rescue scene.

Except this wasn't a Hollywood movie—she couldn't count on the inevitable happy ending waiting smugly at the end of the script.

Fear and humiliation gripped her, a sudden wave of panic that choked the air out of her lungs and left her thrashing about the floor, fighting to breathe through the cotton cloth that clung to her damp face. To keep from suffocating, she turned over on her back and lay still. Breathe deeply, evenly.

Concentrate on the pain.

Frustrated, she began to cry. Tears stung her swollen eyes. She cried until she had no more tears left and then sobbed silently to herself. No matter how it looked, the situation wasn't hopeless, she continued to tell herself. She would think of something, as she always had, even in the most difficult of times.

Calmer now, she cleared her head, remembering how sadistically Reno and his friends had treated her. After tightening the hood, they taped her hands and feet, and then someone had thrown her over his shoulder like a rolled-up carpet and carried her back to the shed. There he dropped her heavily on the floor and prodded her with his foot. One of them climbed on top of her and ripped open her blouse, mauling her breasts with hands so rough they felt like sand paper. Then he pulled at her pants, pushing them down just far enough to get his hand over her vagina and his fingers inside her. Then he laughed, as though brutalizing her was a big joke, a form of recreation.

What sounded like an argument ensued, with Reno raising his voice and telling the others to get the hell out. Then the door slammed closed and a padlock clicked shut outside.

She heard Reno say, "Wait until dark, then take her out on the road to Two Wells. You know what to do." The others laughed, just as they'd done while kicking her.

It was then that she understood the gravity of her situation. They were going to kill her, just as they had Michael. She was about to die.

Don't think about that now, she told herself. Don't think about anything. Fight. She had to fight.

Though her wrists ached, she tried to roll over, arching her back slightly so as not to put too much pressure on her bleeding hands. She rolled to her left. Once, then twice, bumping into a large metal object. An overturned wheelbarrow, she determined.

Desperate, she clawed at the hollow metal with her fingers. It was no good. She couldn't find a sharp edge, so she gave up and rolled the other way. Three, four times she rolled before coming to rest against what felt like a heavy wooden crate. It would have to do. Shifting positions, she began to rub the tape against the edge of the crate, slowly at first and then frantically as she began to despair that the wood was too dull to cut the tape.

Several times she paused to catch her breath and to remind herself to slow down. Take it easy, don't panic—that was the key. Finally she felt the tape began to give. She kept sawing, up and down against the splintered wood, ignoring the pain that shot up her arms into her shoulders. Furiously she worked, using the full force of her body now, twisting and turning and pushing until at last the tape snapped and she fell back panting on the hard floor.

She lay still for several moments, waiting for any indication that someone had heard her movements. When she was satisfied, she lifted her body just enough to pull her cramped arms out from under her. Her fingers still numb, she fumbled with the cotton hood covering her head, pulling at the drawstring. No use. She had to open and close her fingers to bring back the circulation. Then she tried again, this time finding the knot and gradually working the string loose.

Ripping off the hood gave her a sense of exhilaration, as did spitting out the handkerchief that gagged her. All that remained was the tape around her ankles, and she went to work on that with a rush of energy, removing her sandals and then twisting and turning her feet until she loosened the tape enough to slip one foot out of the loop and then the other.

She'd done it.

Now that she was free, her wrists didn't seem to hurt quite so much. Fumbling to put her sandals back on, she glanced around the dark shed. A narrow building, partly underground, with the only light coming from two windows, one in front next to the padlocked door, and the other on the side of the building, just behind the wheelbarrow. As her eyes adjusted to the semi-darkness, she could see the stone walls and wooden rafters overhead. A dank smell came from behind her, where the shed opened onto a tunnel dug into the hillside. The iron bars on the windows would make her escape more difficult.

She hobbled painfully over to the front window and looked out at the back of the trading post some twenty or thirty yards down the hill toward the highway. No sign of activity around the building or what little of the parking lot she could see. Would someone hear her and come to her rescue if she screamed? Too risky, she decided, unless she actually saw a car driving into the parking lot and knew for sure that someone would be within hearing distance.

Someone other than Reno and his friends.

Standing at the window made her ankles ache. She needed to keep moving to prevent them from getting stiff. She hobbled over to the side window, carefully moving the wheelbarrow out of her way. From the window she could see Reno's gray van parked alongside the shed. On top of the van a rusted metal rack held a stack of long teepee poles, the pine and aspen saplings stripped of their bark and peeled white, their tips extending a good ten feet over the front of the van.

Beyond the van, she saw a distant ridge of rock, splashed red by the late afternoon light. The light reminded her of the time. It was getting late.

Up close, she examined the iron grating on the windows. The bars were maybe ten inches apart. The gap was wide enough for a very small adult like herself to squeeze through. Just looking at the bars convinced her that she could do it, climb up on the wheelbarrow and pull herself through the bars.

Once outside, she could make a run for the ridge and then circle around to the 7-Eleven and get help. All that lay between her and freedom was the window, an old-fashioned sash window open a couple of inches for ventilation.

She placed her hands under the window frame and pushed up. Nothing. She tried again. This time it budged, squeaking loud enough for her to worry about the noise. Trying to be quiet, she gradually eased the window open wide enough to allow her to crawl through.

Working quickly now, she dragged the wheelbarrow up to the window, grabbed hold of the bars and poked her head through.

Almost too easy. She paused, reconsidering. Most likely she would never have another chance to look around...to find evidence, to get a good look at what Reno was looting. A few more minutes might not put her in any immediate danger. She checked her watch. Five o'clock. Sunset was still a couple of hours away. Deciding to give it a try, she stepped down from the wheelbarrow and began a systematic examination of the shed.

Shovels and picks leaned against the front wall, next to the door. But along the far wall she found a long metal workbench, cluttered with an assortment of tools and small paintbrushes, along with scattered bottles of cleaning solvent. Placed in separate cardboard boxes, several cracked and dirt-coated pots waited to be cleaned. A crude operation, she decided, from the look of things. What she'd expect from a looter like John Reno.

Toward the back of the shed a series of steps descended into a dark cave-like room. She started down the uneven steps, feeling with her toes in order to keep her balance. The moldy smell of moist earth grew stronger as she entered the underground room, where the feeble light from above dissolved in the subterranean gloom.

Dark shadows appeared ahead of her, the vertical forms becoming more distinct as she came closer. They were round wooden beams that supported the roof of the cave. And she saw something else, an electrical wire that looped around the poles. Following the wire, she came to a bare bulb hanging overhead and reached for the chain, wanting to finish her business quickly and get out of here.

When she pulled the chain, a flash of yellow light illuminated the cave. What she saw shocked her at first. There were rows of human skulls arranged neatly on a worktable. All sizes of human skulls, some with the lower jaw and some without. A bad omen, this. Pausing a moment, she reminded herself that human skulls were nothing to be afraid of. The dead could not harm her. Only the living.

Even so, she averted her eyes as she walked around the table to a set of gray metal shelves stacked with dozens of pots Reno and his friends had looted. Pots already cleaned and repaired, waiting to be sold. Everything from small cup-size bowls to large water jars with handles. Most were Anasazi gray-on-black, with serrated lines and arrows, but she also noticed some that looked like the rose-colored St. John's Polychrome variety and others she could not identify. Together the pots would be worth a small fortune.

Off to the side she found a wooden bin filled with newer objects, most of them Zuni. There were baskets, kachina dolls, mudhead masks, and what looked like the helmet-like mask of a Shalako costume.

The sight infuriated her. For an outsider to possess the garb of a sacred Shalako would be the ultimate violation of Zuni religion. Filled with dread, she examined the ornate mask, touching its white wooden face and black leather eyes, its turquoise-colored buffalo horns.

Suddenly a noise upstairs caught her attention. The sound, a metallic click, seemed to come from the front of the shed. Her spirits sank. By delaying too long she'd put herself in danger. She needed to get out of here fast.

Hurrying, she reached up and turned off the overhead light, plunging the cave into darkness. Gradually her eyes adjusted, allowing her to see the uneven steps dug out of the hillside and the dim swath of light at the top. Freedom.

Moving through the thick wooden beams, she began to climb the steps one at a time, listening for any sound. She feared the worst, expecting Reno to be waiting for her at the top of the stairs.

No movement, no noise, only the sound of her own rapid breathing, the air sucking in and out of her lungs in frightened little gasps, like whispers in the dark.

When she came to the top, she held her breath for a moment. Only after her eyes scanned every inch of the gloomy shed did she begin to relax. She found the front door closed tight, the discarded tape scattered about the dirt floor, everything exactly as she'd left it. No sign of Reno or his friends. No voices outside.

Had she imagined the noise? Feeling bolder, she moved quickly over to the side window and climbed up on the wheelbarrow. Outside, the coast looked clear. She saw only the gray van and the ridge beyond, beckoning her to safety. All she had to do was climb through the open window.

Exactly as she'd planned.

But when she reached for the iron bars, the door suddenly flew open and slammed against the wall. The force of the blow sent shockwaves across the entire shed. She screamed, lost her balance, and fell backwards onto the hard dirt floor. The fall knocked the wind out of her lungs and sent bursts of bright colors shooting across her field of vision. She couldn't breathe.

Struggling to sit up, she tried to focus her eyes. A blurry Reno stood in the doorway, his tall gangly body framed by the late-afternoon light. She saw his red, drooping mustache, his skinny toothpick legs. Everything about him terrified her.

"Come here." He moved toward her with a cruel, leering smile.

Behind him came the Zuni woman, nearly as tall as Reno, her body shrouded by her red blanket dress.

Without warning, Reno pounced on her. He ripped off her torn silk blouse and grabbed roughly at her breasts. Then he began removing her pants. Screaming, she could smell Reno's sour breath as his mouth smothered hers.

While she lay pinned under Reno, the Zuni woman kicked the door closed violently. Then she tipped back her head and let loose a laugh so deep that it startled her.

Part Three: Cibola

19

He slowed down entering Whitewater, turning into the driveway of Whitewater Zuni Traders. Loose gravel kicked up under the spinning wheels of the Plymouth, splattering against the bottom of the heavy chassis. As he drove up the gradual incline, he could feel Antonio's body grow tense. The big man sat rigid in the passenger's seat, one hand propped against the dash and the other holding the door handle. Just looking at Antonio made him tense, too.

When they pulled into the parking lot, Antonio reached down and unsnapped his holster strap.

"Hey, Antonio...relax, will you?"

Not listening, Antonio opened the door, ready to jump out.

He parked between a Ford pickup and a Jeep Cherokee and then looked in the rearview mirror, waiting for the highway patrol car following them. Too nervous, Antonio didn't bother to wait. Jumping out, he walked stiffly to the dusty red pickup and checked the cab and then headed for the Cherokee, circling the vehicle like a bird of prey hunting.

He waited until he saw officer Roybal pull in behind him. Then he opened his door and stepped outside, quickly getting his bearings. First, the trading post, an ugly gray stone building that looked like an old gas station, without the gasoline pumps. The iron bars on the windows made it even uglier. Off to the side, a mobile home. In back, another ugly stone building, this one a small shed or dugout. And there, parked next to the shed, he saw John Reno's van. Road Chief's van.

The van was just as he imagined it, with teepee poles stacked on top, ready for the next peyote meeting. The canvas teepee cover would be in the rear of the van, along with the other paraphernalia needed to hold a peyote ceremony. Toss in Reno and a couple of his friends and presto, the van would become a Native American Church on wheels. Have peyote, will travel—any time, any place.

Except the bogus show Reno put on didn't really have anything to do with the Native American Church. It was only a masquerade, a convenient way for people like Reno and Soto to steal from the Hispanic and Native American communities. Reno the supplier, Soto the dealer. Until Reno learned the hard way, thanks to Santeros Artesana, that Soto was stealing from his own partner.

The state trooper came over to join him, one hand on his nightstick and the other itching toward his holster. He led the way down the flagstone walk to the front entrance. Ignoring the "Closed" sign in the window, he tried the door and found it unlocked. The heavy wooden door creaked on its hinges. He pushed it open and walked into a dark, dingy room that smelled like stale air and rotting wood. Not exactly what he expected to find. Like an old garage filled with junk. How else describe a haphazard arrangement of cowboy memorabilia—saddles, stirrups, branding irons, and other garage sale items dangling from long nails pounded into the pine walls.

To get a closer look, he walked across the room to a glass display case. Inside the case he saw a few pieces of pottery. They looked old and valuable, though he had no way of knowing for sure. No signs, no price tags, nothing to indicate origin or value. Some way to run a business.

Except Whitewater Zuni Traders wasn't a business, just a front for Reno's other, more lucrative enterprises.

"Anyone here?" he shouted.

Footsteps in the back room provided the answer. Someone was coming.

He moved to the center of the room and waited.

Two men came out of an open archway behind the counter, their faces hidden in shadow until one of them flipped a light switch and turned on the bare bulb that dangled overhead. The men looked like manual laborers. T-shirts and dirty jeans. Like they'd just come in from a construction site. Or a dig. Whatever they'd been doing, it wasn't working inside a trading post.

"We're closed," one of the men said from behind the counter, a short powerfully built Anglo with a blond crew cut. His partner, an Hispanic, stood back in the protection of the archway, a thin emaciated man with a craggy face and long, stringy hair the color of dirt.

He ignored the comment. "Are you John Reno?"

"No, he ain't here right now...I told you, we're closed," the man with the crew cut said, glancing over at Antonio and Roybal. Uneasy, in spite of his bravado, at the sight of two armed cops blocking the front door.

He frowned. "When will Reno be back?"

"I don't know. I think he went up to Gallup. Maybe tomorrow. Why?"

"We're looking for a woman by the name of Wanda LeClair. She came here earlier today. What happened to her?"

At the mention of the LeClair woman, the thin man's lower jaw dropped. Not much, but just enough to tell him what he needed to know.

The two men didn't appear to be armed. No heavy artillery visible. But that didn't mean they didn't have a little something tucked away, a sweet little .22 pistol, for example. Like the one used to kill Soto.

Mr. crew cut shook his head. "Don't know what you're talking about. Never heard of anyone by that name. Who is she?"

"The manager of Sabado Indian Arts in Santa Fe. Small woman, with strawberry blond hair. Drives a Honda Accord."

"Sorry, I can't help you." The man shook his head.

"We don't see many Santa Fe types up here," the thin man said, laughing from the safety of the archway.

"Yeah," crew cut said. "Why would she come here?"

"Good question," he snapped, staring at the thin man until the stupid smile disappeared from his sunburned face.

A tense silence filled the room. Antonio and Roybal moved farther apart. Thin man wasn't smiling now.

"You won't mind if I look around." It was a statement, not a question.

He looked back over his shoulder. "Roybal, keep our friends company while Antonio and I get some fresh air, okay?"

Roybal nodded, his eyes fastened on the two punks.

He marched around the side of the building. Just as he did, the sun disappeared behind the western ridge. Having fallen into shadow, the ridge looked like a great wall of black rock.

The wind began to pick up, blowing dust into his eyes and mouth. He paused, momentarily blinded by the dust. He could taste the grains of sand in his mouth, and something else. The bitter taste of ash. He smelled it now, a trace of smoke from a fire somewhere nearby. When he started again, heading for Reno's gray van, he heard Antonio calling out behind him, near the back of the trading post.

"Over here," Antonio shouted.

Antonio stood beside a rusted fifty-gallon barrel. A barrel used to burn trash.

"What is it?" he asked, coming up to the barrel.

Antonio motioned to the charred remains inside the barrel—tin cans, bottles, plastic containers, newspapers, and pieces of wood thrown all together and still smoldering.

"You see it?"

"See what?"

Antonio reached down and picked up a piece of charred wood about the size of a man's forearm. Light wood, partially burned by the fire. A familiar shape, even in its present condition.

He nodded, examining the shrouded head of an ahayu:da, snapped off cleanly from its body.

"Must be another copy."

"Yeah, the one Soto gave back to Reno," he said. "Soto tried to pass it off as the original. That's why he was killed."

"But Santeros Artesana had the original," Antonio said, confused.

"Yeah, because Soto gave it to Santeros Artesana to copy. They were working with Soto until they decided he was cheating them...just like Reno found out Soto was cheating him."

Then he grabbed a stick from the ground and poked at the coals inside the barrel, disturbing a bundle of smoldering newspapers. His poking produced a cloud of ashes and a thin wisp of smoke that curled around the lip of the charred barrel.

"Forget it." He dropped the stick into the barrel.

When he turned to go, he thought he saw movement over by the mobile home, a big white trailer that looked new, or close to it. It was some twenty or thirty yards north of the trading post, beyond a dusty patch of weeds and a set of clothesline poles.

"Why don't you check that out," he said.

"What?"

"You didn't see that...over behind the mobile home?"

"See what?" Antonio asked. He sounded irritated.

"Never mind."

"Probably a skinwalker." Antonio grunted in disgust.

They followed a set of deep ruts in the dirt, climbing a gradual slope to the shed. Built out of the same ugly gray stone with bars on the windows, just like the trading post. Bars everywhere.

Reno's van, a light gray GMC, looked older and more dilapidated the closer they came. It had a cracked windshield, dented fenders, and splotches of red primer showing. The long teepee poles that sagged over its front end gave the van a tired, drooping look.

Suddenly the wind picked up again. He raised his arm to cover his eyes. He heard Antonio cursing behind him. Fuck this, fuck that.

Then, just as suddenly, the wind died down. Now the air was perfectly still. Silent. He could hear himself breathing, out of breath from the exertion of walking up the hill.

He paused to get his breath and then looked into the cluttered van. Through the rear window he saw a white canvas teepee cover, folded to the size of a bale of hay and thrown on top of a spare tire. Wooden stakes and a length of half-inch rope lay beside the canvas, as did a wooden crate containing the props required to stage a peyote ceremony—the drum and rattle, the water pail and cup, the eagle bone whistle, the white leather pouch filled with powdered cedar, and an assortment of hawk and eagle feather fans.

And he saw something else, a hunting rifle, with scope, inside an open rife case. Looked like an old reliable Winchester

M70 with .30-06 ammo, good for hunting big game or for taking pot shots long distance at Jacoñita.

Wouldn't you know? He should have suspected.

No bag of peyote was visible, but that came as no surprise. Reno wouldn't leave a bag of peyote out in plain sight.

Nothing else in the van interested him at the moment. He wanted to find Wanda LeClair. Before it was too late.

Stepping back, he heard muffled sounds coming from inside the shed.

He could hear muted voices and something else. A struggle? Antonio moved first. He ducked below the ends of the teepee poles and walked toward the front of the shed. Just as he did the door to the shed opened and a tall man with a red handlebar mustache stepped out and then closed the door behind him. A cowboy type, the man was wearing a silver belt buckle the size of a softball and a black pearl-button shirt stuffed carelessly, too carelessly, into his jeans. He looked dangerous.

"What do you boys want?" the man demanded, moving cautiously as he approached Antonio. His pasty white face looked bloodless against his red hair. Like a death mask, ringed with fire.

He circled the van so that he could get a clear view of the front of the shed. "Are you John Reno?"

The man looked from him to Antonio, then back to him again. "I'm John Reno. What do you want?"

"We're looking for Wanda LeClair. The woman who came here this afternoon. Where is she?"

"She's not here." The tension was showing on his pale face. His long arms hung limply at his sides.

He persisted. "Small, blond woman. You took her car down to the pueblo and tried to dump it there. Remember?"

Reno took a small step backwards. "No. She left by herself. I don't know where she went."

While he spoke, the door to the shed opened and a tall Zuni woman stepped out. An odd looking woman, too tall for a Zuni. Long face and shoulder-length black hair. Wrapped in a red blanket.

Reno seemed to feel the Zuni woman behind him, to take

confidence from her presence. "Ask my wife if you don't believe me," he said. "The woman left early this afternoon."

He turned to the Zuni woman. "Is that right?"

The Zuni woman ignored him, moving slowly away from Reno, out toward the open yard.

The Zuni's slow but constant movement troubled him. As did the blank expression on her face. Didn't she speak?

"Stay where you are!" Antonio barked, not bothering to hide his hostility.

But the woman kept moving forward, her eyes clouded. As if she were in a trance, unable to see or hear them. Closer and closer to him.

Suddenly the door to the shed burst open and a woman staggered outside, disheveled and covered with dirt, and trying to pull up her pants as she ran. He recognized the bruised, swollen face of Wanda LeClair, her strawberry blond hair now clotted with dirt. Her silk blouse had been ripped open in front, revealing her round white breasts underneath.

"Berdache!" she screamed, trying to make them understand while struggling to free her wrists from a loose strand of duct tape. "Berdache!"

"It's the woman!" Antonio shouted.

Then he understood. The fourth man in the van. What a fool he'd been.

He vaguely recalled that berdaches were Zuni men who dressed like women and who combined the social and work roles of both sexes. An ancient tradition at Zuni. Not so common today.

At the peyote ceremony the berdache had pretended to be Reno's wife, Peyote Woman. It all made sense now.

Reno, surprised by Wanda LeClair's appearance, jumped back toward the shed.

The berdache also moved. He saw the hand dart inside the folds of his red blanket dress.

Lunging, he caught the berdache with a shoulder to the chest. The force of the blow knocked the wind out of the berdache and sent him sprawling backwards. He landed on top, feeling the hard metal of the pistol pinned between their bodies. The barrel pushed against his belly and then worked its way lower, smashing against his hip bone as they flailed about on the ground.

He panicked, unable to wrestle the gun out from under the twisted blanket. He dug his right knee into the berdache's groin until he heard him cry out sharply. And still the berdache fought, pushing his forearm against his throat.

Choking, he could only continue kicking at the berdache's groin. Trying to get at the gun. No use. He couldn't get under the red blanket.

Then everything seemed to happen at once.

Wanda LeClair sprinted toward the ridge of rock behind them, taking advantage of the confusion.

Reno dashed into the shed, Antonio sprinting after him.

Then he heard the muffled pop of the pistol, like a firecracker on the Fourth of July.

He held his breath, waiting for the first jolt of pain. None came.

Someone moaned. The berdache.

He felt the berdache's body go limp beneath him. As he tried to lift himself, the berdache screamed in pain.

"What? Where is it?" he asked, still fumbling with the blanket. He struggled to pull the dress up over the man's hips. As he did the shiny black pistol spilled out onto the ground.

Finding the wound took precious seconds because the berdache screamed whenever he pulled too hard. But he persisted, working more carefully, until he exposed the wound. He found a small bullet hole in the man's upper thigh, and a jagged gash above the knee where the bullet, after shattering the leg bone had exited. Bright red blood boiled up out of the gash and pooled on the ground below the shattered leg.

"Jesus Christ." He pulled off his belt and tightened it around the man's thigh just above the wound. There was blood everywhere, all over both of them.

He fumbled with the tourniquet, ignoring the bulge in the man's jockey shorts.

The berdache, his eyes closed, made a low moaning sound.

"You're going to be okay," he reassured him.

While he stayed with the berdache, he heard Roybal shouting from down by the trading post.

A moment later Roybal ran halfway up the hill, waving

his .38 out in front of him. "You need help? Is everything under control?"

"Yeah. Call an ambulance. And make it quick."

He glanced at the berdache's weapon. Looked like a Smith and Wesson, double-action .22 caliber. The most rudimentary of weapons. But sophisticated enough to do some serious damage to a man's leg.

Sophisticated enough to kill Soto.

He imagined the killing. The berdache stepping outside for the Midnight Water Call, removing his blanket and slipping on the wolf mask, then pushing José Padilla back through the door of the teepee. Soto running blindly toward the arroyo, and the berdache stealing across the desert to Soto's Porsche...to wait for his prey.

After the murder, the berdache would have returned to the teepee, put on his blanket dress, and joined the others. As simple as that.

Shaking his head, he listened to the racket coming from inside the shed. Angry words first, then shouting, and finally the sound of glass and wood shattering. Maybe Reno was tougher than he looked, because normally it wouldn't take Antonio this long to subdue whatever poor bastard tried to resist arrest.

Suddenly from inside the shed he heard the sound of a shovel hitting something hard and hollow, like someone's head. "Motherfucker!" came a retort. After a tremendous crash, the shed fell silent. Only the moans of the berdache disturbed the late afternoon silence.

Then a strange sound caught Fernando's attention. A scraping sound. He began to worry, until he saw Antonio step out of the doorway dragging the unconscious body of Reno behind him. Dragging the body by one foot, as a hunter might drag the carcass of a deer.

The left side of Antonio's face was bleeding.

"What happened?" he asked.

"The sonofabitch hit me with a shovel," Antonio snorted.

He shook his head. Not a good move on Reno's part.

Antonio dropped Reno's foot and reached for his handcuffs. He flipped Reno over and cuffed the gangly hands behind his back. Then he kicked Reno hard in the ribs. "He'll come around soon enough."

"I pity the man when he does."

Antonio grinned, wiping the blood from his face with a handkerchief.

"Roybal went to call an ambulance. Can you keep an eye on these two while I go after the woman?"

"No problem," Antonio said, coming over to look at the berdache's wound. "They won't be going anywhere."

When Reno moaned and started to move his arms, Antonio stepped on the back of his head and pushed his face down into the dirt. "Shut the fuck up!"

He hadn't realized the extent of his own injuries until he tried to walk. The back of his neck throbbed, his hips and rib cage ached, and his legs would hardly bend. He wiped his bloody hands on his jeans and took a step, then another, trying to loosen his stiff joints.

Enough was enough. He was too getting too old for this.

"You okay?" Antonio asked.

"Yeah, sure, I'm okay."

Beside the van he stopped for a moment, looking for where Wanda LeClair might have gone. Over the ridge, he supposed. But how? Squinting, his tired eyes scoured the landscape, until they found the faint lines of a jeep trail leading to a gap in the ridge. Rocks and rattlesnakes. Just what he needed.

If she would only stop running away from him, he wouldn't have to worry about rocks and rattlesnakes. He limped toward the trail, taking his time so as not to fall.

Halfway up the trail he stopped to rest his cramping legs. Though he desperately craved a cigarette, he decided to wait until later. No time for pleasure now, not with the western sky already streaked with crimson. Dusk would soon make it all but impossible to find the woman.

Limping along slowly, he eventually made it to the top, stumbling through the narrow pass littered with loose rocks that had fallen from the cliffs onto the trail. As he came out into the open air he felt the wind strike his face. The burst of fresh, cool wind invigorated him momentarily. The smell of approaching rain hung in the air like a promise.

Spread out in front of him he saw a vast shadowy panorama of gray sagebrush flats dotted with distant black mesas gradually fading into the purple horizon. To the south, Zuni. To the west and north, Navajo and Hopi country.

Zuni and Navajo and Hopi. As far as the eye could see. As it had been for hundreds of years.

Then he spotted her sitting on an outcropping of rock up ahead. Not wanting to frighten her, and conscious of the fact that he was covered in blood, he walked out in the open along the edge of the ridge. As he came closer he saw her holding something in her hands, what looked like a jagged rock. The sight of her holding a rock puzzled him at first. Then it occurred to him that she was afraid of him and preparing to defend herself. Who could blame her?

When he stepped on to the outcropping of rock, keeping his distance, she turned to face him. She tugged at her torn blouse, trying to cover her nakedness.

He stared at her, not knowing where to begin. He felt awkward, like an intruder.

"We have Reno in our custody," he said finally. "He won't hurt you now. An ambulance is on the way...I mean, if you need help—"

She looked at him fiercely. "What do you want from me? Are you going to arrest me too, because of what Michael did?"

He backed away, as though she had slapped him across the face. "No, I just want to make sure you're okay."

"No, I'm not okay," she said. "I'll never be okay."

"Do you need medical attention?"

She looked down at her torn, dirty clothing. "I don't think so."

"The medics will be here soon."

She shook her head and looked away. Only then did she turn to him. "Can you help me to my car?"

"Yes," he said weakly, relieved that he could do something to help. "Thank you," he said.

The woman stared at him, uncomprehending.

20

While he waited, he opened the top drawer of his desk and took out a fresh legal pad. Most likely he would need no more than one sheet of paper, but he wanted to be prepared just in case he got carried away with a sense of righteous indignation. Finding the proper way to begin proved to be the difficult part. He'd never actually sat down to write a resignation letter, in spite of the fact that he'd threatened to retire so often that no one around the office took him seriously anymore. Well, he would show them who was serious.

Choosing a felt-tip pen, he addressed the letter to Larry Stuart, Chief of Police, and then found himself staring at a blank page. Must be writer's block. To create some psychic space, he cleared the center of his desk, pushing the ashtray and the Burger King cups toward the edges of the desk. Much better. He felt the words coming in one big rush.

"After thirty years of service, I hereby resign from the Santa Fe Police Department, effective immediately," he wrote.

But wait. Shouldn't he state a reason for his resignation? One miserable sentence didn't seem sufficient for an official letter of resignation. So he tried again on another sheet of paper.

"Because of my advancing age," he wrote, then decided against using his age as an excuse. He didn't want to put it all on himself and let Stuart and the others off the hook so easily. So he crossed out "my advancing age" and added "all the bullshit." There. "Because of all the bullshit, I hereby resign from the Santa Fe Police Department, effective immediately." No, he didn't like that either. Sounded like sour grapes. The complaints of a disgruntled employee. No one would take him seriously.

While he pondered what to do, the phone rang. "Do you want to talk to Fidel Rodriguez from the *Independent* on line one?" Linda asked.

"No, tell him I'm out," he said. Which wasn't totally false, since he had a coffee appointment at the Great Burrito Company in fifteen minutes.

"Oh, what the hell, I'll take it," he said, changing his mind. He hadn't returned any of Fidel's calls since getting back from Zuni three days ago. He'd made sure to stop in Tesuque to tell Robert Naranjo and Billy Suino the news, but he hadn't taken the time to call Fidel.

"What can I do for you?"

"Some information," Fidel answered. "I'm told that Soto's will is likely to hold up in Probate Court. That Judge Baca feels satisfied the signature on the will is Soto's, even if there might be some irregularity with the witnesses. Can you verify that?"

"I hear the same thing. You know as much as I do about it—I've been busy with the murder investigation."

"Baca seems to think the handwriting experts Raoul Garcia hired were convincing," Fidel added.

He frowned. "I bet they were."

"What do you mean?"

"Nothing. Really, I haven't been following the legal battle over Soto's estate. But I bet Garcia and Wanda LeClair make a formidable pair."

Fidel laughed. "What about Padilla and the Santeros Artesana boys? Why did you release them without filing charges?"

"Don't blame me. I don't file charges. The prosecutor does that."

"Okay, why didn't Steve Chabot file charges?"

He sighed. "What would he charge them with? Copying the ahayu:da?"

"What do you mean?"

"Look," he said impatiently. "Reno stole the ahayu:da and gave it to Soto to sell. Soto cheated Reno. He took it to Santeros Artesana and had them make a copy to give back to Reno, pretending it was the original. Then Santeros Artesana cheated

Soto in exactly the same way. They kept the original and gave Soto two fakes.

"Once they had the original, Santeros Artesana continued to make copies, which they intended to sell with the assistance of José Padilla. To cover themselves, and to hopefully get rid of Soto, they sent letters to John Reno and the Zuni Tribal Council informing them that Soto was trying to sell the ahayu:da around Santa Fe.

"When Reno discovered this, he realized that Soto had given him a fake ahayu:da and kept the original for himself. Except, of course, that Soto didn't have the original either. Santeros Artesana did. So when Reno and his berdache killed Soto during the peyote ceremony, they never found the real ahayu:da."

"Like a food chain," Fidel said.

"More like a chain of thieves, all trying to cheat each other."

"One more thing. What happened to Soto's second ahayu:da, the one he didn't give to Reno?"

"That's the one José Padilla tried to sell in Taos," he said. "Most likely he got it at the peyote ceremony."

"So it worked out perfectly for everyone concerned—except John Reno and the berdache."

"And Michael Soto."

"And Michael Soto," Fidel repeated. "Oh, and what about Jose Padilla?"

"Don't know yet. Cabot hasn't decided. Probably just a fine, since all he really did was try to sell a fake ahayu:da."

"Got it. Thanks. That's all I need for my story."

Hanging up the phone, he glanced at his resignation letter and cringed. He couldn't give the chief such a pathetic, whining letter. No way. He would have to take it home and ask for Estelle's help. Estelle had more imagination than he did. She would know what to say and how to say it properly, without attributing the resignation to his shortcomings or departmental bullshit.

Tearing up the letter gave him a sense of relief, as if he'd just escaped a close call. Maybe he wouldn't resign, after all. Stay on for another five years, just to irritate Chief Stuart and all the young turks waiting to take his place. Why not?

He grabbed his emergency pack of cigarettes and then

headed down the hallway to the front desk. Business was slow this morning. He could tell by looking at Linda as she huddled over a crossword puzzle, an expression of exasperation on her face.

He walked outside into the sunshine. Already hot, but not a cloud in the bright blue sky. Hard to believe another summer was almost over. He hated the thought of winter.

Fumbling with his sunglasses, he watched a string of cars drive down Washington Avenue toward the Plaza. Labor Day weekend. The tourists were gathering for one final fling before heading back home to watch their home videos and pay off their credit cards so they could come again next year.

Halfway to the Great Burrito Company he caught a glimpse of the Plaza. The flashy red sign in the door of Sabado Indian Arts announced in big bold letters: "Reopening Soon. Under New Ownership."

Then he saw Wanda LeClair waiting for him at one of the sidewalk tables up ahead. Her face looked much better, no longer swollen or discolored. But as he came closer and saw the black eye, he realized that she had covered her bruises with make-up.

Up close, she looked about as bad as he felt. He still walked with a limp. His hips hurt like hell, and his ribs ached when he breathed. He felt like he'd been in an automobile accident, a rollover.

"Detective Lopez," she said, standing up to greet him. "Thanks for coming."

He nodded. "How are you feeling?"

"Much better," she said. "Please. Sit down."

The low-cut denim dress made her look very young. And very sexy. He hadn't realized how sexy.

He sat in the chair next to hers. Overhead, a red and white striped table umbrella shaded them from the sun.

"I wanted to thank you for what you did—" she began, lowering her eyes as her voice trailed off.

Her call this morning had taken him by surprise. Still, he'd agreed to meet her for coffee, curious as to how she was doing. He felt somehow responsible for what had happened to her at Whitewater. He should have involved her more in the investigation, kept her informed. He should have warned her about Reno.

"What I mean to say is that I'm sorry for the way I reacted to you," she said, trying again. "Later, after I calmed down, I understood that you were only trying to help me. Actually, you saved my life. I owe you an apology. I don't want you to think I'm ungrateful."

"No problem. I didn't take it personally. You were upset after what had happened. Who could blame you? Actually, I think I owe you an apology. I should have warned you about Reno. I mistrusted you at first, thinking you were working with Soto, just another gallery owner...or gallery manager. That was my mistake, and I'm sorry for it."

"Well, we all made mistakes. When I think that I drove all the way out to Whitewater assuming I could convince—or force—Reno to stop looting and selling tribal objects...I can't imagine what I was thinking. It sounds so ridiculous when I say it now. You were right to suspect me."

"Still, you could have been killed, like Soto. I should have warned you."

When the waitress came to take their orders, he felt grateful for the distraction.

"Iced tea, please," she said.

He ordered his usual, coffee with extra cream and sugar.

"I saw your new sign at Sabado Indian Arts."

She laughed. "It's a bit garish, I know. It looked better in the drawing." She paused a moment to reflect. "You know, when I signed my name as a witness to Soto's will, I had no idea what—"

He stopped her. "You don't need to explain. Nobody's accusing you of anything. Your signature made no difference. The will would have stood up in court anyway. Really. Soto had no family."

"How sad," she said, sipping her tea.

"I don't mean to upset you, but you will be asked to testify against Reno and the berdache."

She tensed at the mention of Reno.

"I guess you knew that," he said, for lack of anything better to say.

She nodded. "Something still bothers me about all this. I know the berdache killed Michael...and might have killed me.

But Reno controlled him like a puppet. It doesn't seem fair that of all the people involved, all the looters and profiteers, only the Zuni goes to jail."

"Not exactly. Reno will do some time, at least three to five years. Then he'll be back at Whitewater."

"Back to looting," she said, the disapproval evident in her voice.

He frowned. "I'm afraid so. The legal system works in mysterious ways."

She nodded. "Sometimes I see Reno's face. Usually at night, just before I fall asleep. Leering at me."

"Hard to forget a face like that."

"He sexually assaulted me. He would have raped me. He just didn't have time to complete the act."

He agreed. "In which case he would have done more time. As it is... " He shook his head sadly.

"The legal system."

"Yes...exactly."

She crossed her legs at the table and studied his face, as if contemplating a riddle. "Reno and the berdache. Do you think they were...you know, lovers?"

Shrugging, he said, "Yeah, I've been wondering the same thing."

"Not that I have a problem with people who are bisexual or who refer to themselves as a third gender, I don't."

He nodded.

"I know many of the younger Zuni prefer the term 'two spirit' instead of berdache. I like 'two spirit' because it better describes people who combine the social roles of both men and women."

"But you shouted out the word 'berdache' when you warned us back in Whitewater."

"It's true, I did." She sat back in her chair, thinking. "I guess I thought you would recognize the term berdache and not the other."

"Which I did," he said. "And you're right, I wouldn't have understood what you meant by 'two spirit.'"

She looked at him. "But what about them being lovers? What do you think?"

He laughed. "Who knows? I wouldn't presume to judge the berdache, but Reno doesn't strike me as much of anything sexually. If you know what I mean."

She smiled briefly. A half smile. "But they pretended to be married."

"Pretended," he repeated. "As far as I know, a berdache's duties are mostly work related. Social roles, as you say."

"I suppose you're right," she said. "He did seem more interested in hurting than fucking me."

He nodded again and drank his coffee, enjoying the caffeine rush. "Tell me again why you took the two boxes of looted objects to Whitewater. Why didn't you turn them over to the authorities?"

"Good question. I thought Reno would return them to their proper places." She laughed. "Little did I know that Reno and his companions had murdered Michael and weren't about to return anything. Talk about stupidity."

"You had no way of knowing."

"True, but I might have been more careful. I got, I don't know, carried away by the thought of my responsibility for Michael's sordid business. I guess I felt guilty."

He sighed. "Oh yes, I know something about feeling guilty."

"When I think that none of this would have happened if I hadn't met Michael. I don't know, I almost hate him."

"You liked him, didn't you," he said, curious.

"Yes, I did," she said. "You probably wouldn't understand, but I had lived such a lonely life for so long, first at graduate school and then working toward tenure at UNM I just never took time out to have a personal life, and maybe I never really found the right person. Until Michael. We had so much in common... and he was a lot of fun, very outgoing and, well, very handsome," she said, laughing. "As they say, I was a fool for love."

He found himself at a loss for what to say.

"Well...I'm late. I have to run some errands before getting back to the gallery. I'm hoping all this bad publicity doesn't affect the gallery."

"Hey—it's under new ownership," he said, quoting her sign.

She laughed. "We shall see."

When she stood up, he did the same.

“Thanks for coming, and thanks again for what you did at Whitewater,” she said, extending her hand.

He shook the hand limply.

Turning away, she crossed the street and disappeared into the stream of people walking across the Plaza. The new owner of Sabado Indian Arts.

He paused a moment, hoping for one last glimpse of Wanda LeClair and then gave up and headed back to his office. He had a letter of resignation to write.

Readers Guide

1. "That was the problem with Santa Fe—too much history," Detective Lopez thinks to himself early in *Peyote Wolf*. What does he mean by "too much history"?

2. Everyone who attended the peyote ceremony the night Michael Soto was murdered has a different version of what happened at the teepee. When Detective Lopez and Tomas Trujillo question Dora Alvarez of San Ildefonso Pueblo, she tells them that a *skinwalker* or werewolf killed Soto. How do their reactions to the mention of a *skinwalker* differ?

3. In what ways does Detective Lopez function as the moral center of *Peyote Wolf*?

4. Detective Lopez is initially suspicious of Wanda LeClair, Michael Soto's store manager and lover, but does not pursue her involvement in Soto's illegal trade in stolen tribal objects. What might he have done earlier to prevent the violent confrontation at Whitewater?

5. Detective Lopez broods over the sins of his forefathers (the harsh treatment of Pueblo people). How much responsibility do we bear for the sins of our forefathers? How do we heal ancient wounds?

6. Should dealers and gallery owners who sell tribal artifacts of unknown origin or ownership be arrested and charged with a

crime? What about auction houses where these tribal objects sometimes appear? Explain.

7. What are Detective Lopez's motives? Does he always act altruistically? Or does he seem to have his own personal, ulterior motives for his actions? Explain.

8. In his political argument with firebrand lawyer Raoul Garcia, Detective Lopez argues that not every act or confrontation can be racialized. Garcia argues the opposite, that everything comes down to a question of race. Furthermore, he argues that the Anglo judicial system in Santa Fe is corrupt and racist and therefore morally incapable of charging his Hispanic clients with a crime. How do we negotiate this divide?

9. Toward the end of *Peyote Wolf* Wanda LeClair discovers that Michael Soto, her boss and lover, had been buying and selling stolen tribal objects. In an attempt to get rid of the stolen merchandise she devises a plan to return all of the stolen objects to Soto's supplier, the man who looted or otherwise procured the artifacts. Then she threatens to report him to the authorities if he doesn't return them to their rightful owners. In the process she nearly loses her life. What other courses of action might she have taken that might have been less dangerous and resulted in fewer casualties?

www.ingramcontent.com/pod-product-compliance
Lightning Source LLC
Chambersburg PA
CBHW010140030826
48979CB00024B/1078

* 9 7 8 1 6 3 2 9 3 4 2 3 9 *